FOREVER LOVE

BROOKE SUMMERS

FOREVER LOVE
First Edition published in 2020
Text Copyright © Brooke Summers

All rights reserved.

The moral right of the author has been asserted.

Cover Design by Lee Ching of Undercover Designs.
Formatter Kristine Moran of word bunnies.
Editing by Lisa Flynn of Simply Writing.
Proofread by Kristine Moran of word bunnies

No part of this publication may be reproduced, stored in or introduced into a retrieval system, or transmitted, in any form or by any means (electronic, mechanical, photocopying, recording or otherwise), nor be otherwise circulated in any form of binding or cover other than that in which it is published without the prior written permission of the author. Any person who does any unauthorized act in relation to this publication may be liable to criminal prosecution and civil claims for damages.
All characters in this publication are fictitious and any resemblance to real persons, living or dead, is purely coincidental.

❀ Created with Vellum

ONE

Hudson

WALKING INTO THE HOSPITAL, my feet move quickly toward the surgical floor. The smell of sterile cleaning solution assaults my nose. I fucking hate this place, we've spent too much time in hospitals or makeshift ones lately. Every time we come to this damn place, we lose someone. The last one was David's wife, she didn't survive the night, the burns she had were so severe.

Dad's waiting for me as I get there. He looks like shit, he hasn't told me who's been shot, I just needed to get my ass to the hospital. So here I am, and seeing his pale face has me on edge.

"Son..." he begins, his voice shaky.

"Who?" I demand, hating the small talk.

He glances to the floor and then back at me, his eyes glassy as though he's trying not to cry. "There's been two shootings."

"Dad, just fucking spit it out," I tell him. He's pissing me off, I know that whoever it is that's been shot is someone close. I just pray to God that it's not Jagger, Sarah, or Allie.

"Son…" His voice breaks, "Your Ma and Tina were shot."

I blink, my hands balling into fists, "How?"

Dad shakes his head. "Tina was shot first by what I've gathered, she has lost a lot of blood, she wasn't found for a while, your ma, she was shot outside her house. Her neighbors called the cops and an ambulance. She was seen to immediately. They're both in surgery right now."

I shake my head. "Dad, what aren't you telling me?"

He glances away again. "Martin took the two of them out. I've had David search through the security cameras trying to see if he could find out who did this or if there was anything that could lead us to finding out who did it." He's still not telling me something, and I don't have the time to fucking play with this shit.

Pain hits me, he shot my mom. This man is coming after everyone I love. "Fucking hell. How did he know where Mom was? Hell, how did he know where Tina was? Even I didn't know where she was staying."

"I don't know son, I don't even know where your mom's staying. Has he been following you?"

I give my dad a look, and he holds his hands up in surrender. "Look, Son, I wasn't saying that to piss you off, but it's a possibility."

"I know, but he hasn't Dad, I would have known if he were and would have lost him. I can spot a tail a mile off. Every time the cops trail me, I lose them." I laugh. "Fucking hell."

Dad frowns, "What, Son?"

"Before this shit began, I had a tail, a fed, his name was Johnson. A real fucking douche. Anyway, he'd been on my case for months until this shit began, and I've not seen him since."

His eyes narrow. "You think this Johnson's in on this?"

I shrug. "I don't know, but I think the timing is suspect, and I don't believe in coincidences."

"It's time to call the men, have Johnson found," Dad tells me and I sigh. Fucking A, just what we need, kidnapping and threatening a federal agent but it needs to be done.

Pulling out my cell, I call Jagger, he's meant to be with Sarah today but that's about to change. "What?" He grunts and I smile, I've just interrupted something.

"Wrap it up and get your ass over to the club, I'll meet you there in twenty minutes. Gather the men," I tell him. "I'm at the hospital, I'll be leaving soon."

I hear movement and know that he's doing as I ask. "Hospital, what's happened now?"

"I'll tell you when I see you. Call Frankie and get his ass over to your house. Put him on Sarah and Allie."

"Fuck. On it, I'll see you soon." He ends the call, knowing that shits about to go down.

Turning back to Dad I say, "Call me once they're out of surgery, let me know what the doctors say."

He nods. "Son, prepare yourself though. Tina was in bad shape when she was brought in."

"Fuck, just what Mia needs."

"Why don't you call her and bring her here?"

"Dad, until I know for certain, Mia stays at home, she's safe there with Aaron."

"Okay son. I'll call you if I find out anything."

I turn on my heel and walk out of that damn fucking hospital. As soon as I'm outside, fresh air filling my lungs, I dial Aaron to check in on Mia.

"Hey, boss, everything okay?"

"Yeah, how's Mia?"

"I spoke to her once you left, letting her know that I

was here and she told me that she was going to have a shower."

I walk toward my car, my eyes glancing around the parking lot, making sure that I'm aware of who's around me. "Okay, there's a meeting behind held in twenty minutes, you'll not be attending for obvious reasons. What I'm about to say to you does not get repeated."

"Of course, Boss," he replies instantly.

"My mom and Mia's mom were shot, they're both in surgery. Until I know what's happening, I'm not saying anything to Mia, in case Martin's waiting for her to arrive there."

"Makes sense, Boss. Let me know when you want me to bring her to you."

"Thanks, Aaron there's another bit of business but we're on the phone," I tell him, so he knows why I'm not saying anything about it. "I'll talk to you later." I end the call and slide into my car, my mind's focused on how the fuck Martin found out where both Mom and Tina lived, and he's got a thing about going after women. Mia, Lacey, David's wife, Mom, and Tina. It's why I'm glad I had the women and children moved to a safe house. They're out of Martin's reach, they're heavily guarded and as Martin doesn't have an army any more, he's fucked if he ever tried to get to them.

I STRIDE INTO THE CLUB, JAGGER HAS GATHERED EVERY MAN available. The others are at the safe house, and Aaron is with Mia. As soon as I walk in they descend into silence.

"Boss, what's happened?" Alex asks, he's one of the new recruits, I have fifteen of them now. It's great when we're at war and everyone knows it. They want to be with the badass who's offing everyone.

"I had a visit from Aaron this morning at seven o'clock." A murmur goes around my men as they realize he's not here. "He's with Mia right now." That seems to satisfy them. "He informed me that Martin had shot two people this morning or rather late last night. The details are sketchy, but those two people are in surgery right now."

"Who Boss?" Liam asks.

I ignore him for now. "David was tasked with the job of finding out who shot them, searching all cameras in the area and finding clues but once again, Martin fucked up. We know that he personally shot both of them." I nod my head to David in thanks, the man is a fucking monster these days, he's on the hunt, primed for killing and he doesn't give a shit who he kills. He's after blood.

"Tina was shot first, she has lost a lot of blood and we're not sure about her condition." My men straighten their backs as they stand taller. As much of a bitch Tina is, she's my father's wife and that means she's family. "The other person to be shot, was my ma. She was found instantly and the ambulance was called. She, too, is in surgery, again, we're waiting to find out her condition."

"What can we do, Boss?" Rory steps forward, offering himself up.

"Martin is underground, I've been wracking my brain trying to figure out how the fucker has stayed hidden so well, and then I realized something. How many of you remember that fed that was on our case?"

"Johnson?" Jagger asks and I nod. "What about him? He's gone."

"My point exactly, that fucker was on me like he had a fucking hard on for me. Then all of a sudden he's gone, bit of a fucking coincidence that it happened just as this shit happened."

"No such thing," David growls, his arms crossing over his chest.

"My point precisely," I remark, "so I want to know where that fucker is, I want to know what he's doing. I have a hunch that he's working for Martin."

The anger in the room is palpable, the air is sizzling. "Why would he work for him?" Jagger questions.

"I'm not sure, but I have a few ideas. He could have offered me up, giving him everything about my organization along with every crime I committed. Or he could have paid him off. Either way, that shit needs to be stopped."

"What's the plan?" David asks, he's wanting in on the action.

I smile. "There's only one thing to do, we need answers and there's only one way to do that. David, Jagger, Alex and Liam. You are going to find Johnson and bring him to me. I want to know why he backed off and why he's working with Martin."

The four men collectively take a step forward, they're all ready for this. "Take him to the old bar?"

I nod. "Yes, try not to kill anyone while you're getting him."

Each of the men smirk. "We'll try our best," David quips as he walks out of the club.

"I'll call you when we've got him. Let me know if there's any news on your mom or Tina," Jagger says walking past me.

I nod and turn back to the other men in the room. "Have any of you found anything out about Martin or where he may be hiding?"

My question is met with silence.

"Anyone have anything to tell me?" I bite out, what the fuck am I paying them for?

Rory steps forward. "Boss, I did find out something."

"Tell me," I instruct him.

"Boss, well, Martin told us that his mom died recently."

I narrow my eyes. "Yes." I'm wondering where he's going with this.

"Boss, I did some searching and the man and woman who raised Martin are both still alive so I dug up the grave, I took a sample of DNA and had a friend of mine run it. The woman he claimed to be his mom, wasn't. In fact, the woman was young. She was in her teens."

"What the fuck?" I growl. "Who was she and what the fuck happened?"

"Boss, her name was Marline Harrow, she was seventeen and I spoke to her parents. She's been missing for three years, her parents reported her as missing, they say she ran off with her boyfriend."

"Don't tell me, Martin was her boyfriend?" He nods. "Fucking hell, he's the lowest of lows."

"Boss, as I said, his parents are still alive, in fact, I've had my brother keep an eye on them." Rory tells me and I'm surprised he has his brother working for him. He shrugs. "It keeps him out of trouble, so my ma's happy."

I laugh. "You and your brother can accompany my dad there this evening. If your brother wants work, send him my way. I'll have Dad call you once we're finished in the hospital." Just as those words leave me, my cell rings. "I'll talk to you later, use your brains, Martin is hiding from us, we need him found. I don't care how you do it, just do it."

I walk out of the club and answer my cell. "Dad, what's the news?"

"Your ma's out of surgery, they say she's going to be sore but she's going to make a full recovery. She got shot in her chest, but honestly son, she's going to be okay." He reassures me, his voice full of relief.

"Good, what about Tina?"

He silent for a beat. "Still no news, Son she wasn't found for a long time. She's been in surgery for three hours now, maybe more."

Shit, that's not good. "Okay, I'm going home, I'm going to get Mia and we'll be by soon."

"Okay, I'll call if there's any change."

Getting into my car, I call Aaron. "Boss, any news?" I start the engine and put the car into drive.

"Ma's out of surgery, we're waiting on news about Tina. How's Mia?"

"She's okay boss, she's just out of the shower, she called out to me and said she'll be out in a few moments."

Shit, she's not had anything to eat yet. She didn't finish her dinner last night. "Aaron, will you make breakfast, I want her to eat something before we go to the hospital." I slow down as I approach the traffic. Typical San Fran traffic, it's why I hate driving during rush hour.

"Of course boss, anything in particular?"

I don't even have to think, Mia has the same breakfast every day. "Jelly on toast, she loves that."

"Okay, nice and easy. I'll have it ready for her when she comes out, does she drink coffee?"

"No, but have one ready for me. I'll be home in fifteen minutes." If I can get the hell out of this damn traffic.

Thirty minutes later, I'm walking into the house. Mia's sitting at the island in the kitchen eating her breakfast. Aaron's sitting opposite her, eating pancakes. "Coffee?" I ask, as I enter the kitchen fully.

Mia turns to look at me, her face a little pale and the smile she gives me doesn't reach her eyes. "Are you okay?" I ask her as Aaron gets me coffee.

"Yeah, of course, why?" She responds quickly, a little too quickly.

I study her a little harder, her eyes are puffy and red like she's been crying. "Mia, what's wrong?" I ask a little harder this time but she doesn't say anything, she takes a bite of her toast. I leave her be, knowing that she's about to receive some news that's going to upset her, but I'll come back to this in a while.

Aaron hands me the coffee. "Here boss."

"Thanks." I take a sip, "Mia, we need to go to the hospital."

She nods, not saying a word, her eyes on the plate in front of her.

Aaron's eyes widen, I on the other hand am just pissed off. "Mia, did you hear what I said?"

Again, she doesn't look at me. "Yes, we have to go to the hospital."

"Mia, your mom and mine are in the hospital. They've both been shot." I bite out, but she's keeping something from me, she's upset, in a world of her own and she's not talking to me.

She gasps, and finally she looks at me. "Are they okay?"

"Your mom is still in surgery, mine is out but should be okay." I tell her, again, not exactly as soft as it should be. "Once you've finished eating, we'll go. Dad's there now, he's going to call if there's any news."

She gets to her feet. "We need to go now," she tells me her voice rising, she's panicking.

I stand with her, my hands reach out, my fingers framing her face. "Princess listen to me, right now, she's in surgery. There's nothing we can do while she's there."

Tears form in her eyes. "But, she's the only family I have left," she whispers and I pull her into my arms. "I told her to go away yesterday." Her body shaking as she sobs against my shoulder.

"She knows you love her," I tell her quietly. I glance to Aaron and nod my head, he quickly finishes his breakfast and leaves.

"But, I told her that she didn't give a shit about me."

"She knows you didn't mean it."

She pulls back slightly, her eyes wet and puffy. "How long has she been in surgery?"

"Dad said she was brought in before Mom, he thinks she's been in for three hours. Mia, your mom wasn't found right away, she lost a lot of blood before the paramedics got to her."

She pushes away from me and runs toward the bathroom, I blanch at the sound of her throwing up. "Princess?"

"Go away!" she yells as she throws up again.

God, it sounds painful. I walk to the kitchen and get her a glass of water. Waiting outside until she's finished.

A few moments later, she exits out of the bathroom, her face grey and clammy. "Have a sip," I tell her pushing the glass toward her lips.

She has a few sips, and walks toward the kitchen, I follow behind her and watch as she places the glass in the sink. "Can we go please?" she pleads with me and there's no way that I can say no to her.

"Come on, Princess let's go. Hopefully, your mom will be coming out of surgery soon." I take her hand and lead her to the door, making sure that she's steady on her feet. She still looks pale.

"Is your mom okay? Is she badly hurt?" she questions as I help her into the car.

"Yeah baby, she's okay. They said she'll be sore for a while but she's expected to make a full recovery." I walk around to the driver's side and slide in. "It's your mom that we're worried about." I start the engine and reverse out of my driveway.

She nods. "Was it Martin?"

"Yeah, my men found evidence that he was the one to shoot them both."

She begins to sob softly, I reach for her hand and she grabs hold of it tightly. I want to reassure her but I made her a promise, I won't lie to her.

TWO

Mia

I'M A WRECK, there's no other way to describe it. I have no idea what I'm doing, I can't tell Hudson that I'm pregnant not until I know who the father is, I can't do that to him. I'm praying with all my heart and soul that it's Hudson's. I'd be devastated if it wasn't, I'm not sure if I'd be able to keep the baby. I never thought I'd have an abortion but I honestly don't think I'd be able to cope with having a baby that was born out of such brutality.

I grip Hudson's hand tighter, loving the support and comfort he brings me. When he told me that we had to go to the hospital, I was in a world of my own, trying to figure out how to go to the doctors without Hudson knowing but that's not going to happen, I don't think he'd let me go by myself. When he said that both of our mom's had been shot and are in the hospital, it pulled me from my thoughts. I hate Martin with a passion, he hurts everyone and for what? Because his father didn't want him? Because he didn't become the boss? Whatever the reason, he's hurting innocent people. No reason will be good enough for the shit that he's doing. The sooner he's found the better.

"Mia, you're quiet, I don't like it," he tells me softly, he knows that I'm hiding something from him, it's why when he told me about my mom, his tone was full of anger. Hudson is tenacious to say the least, if he wants to know something, he'll do whatever it takes to find out. I won't be able to hold onto my secret for very long, he made me promise him that I wouldn't keep things from him and yet, I'm breaking that promise right now.

"I'm sorry, I'm just trying to process this." I'm not lying, I am but everything is on top of me right now and I'm sinking.

"Don't shut me out, I'm here for you to lean on, for you to vent to, whatever you need, I'm here."

He's being so sweet and yet I have a secret that could break him. "I love you with all my heart," I whisper as I turn to look out the window as the tears slowly cascade down my face.

"Princess, right back atcha. But you're fucking killing me. I know there's something you're not telling me."

I don't say anything, I can't tell him, not just yet. I need to figure out what I want to do.

He parks the car in the parking lot and he gets out. He walks around to the passenger's side and helps me out of the car. "Mia, whatever it is, you can tell me." His fingers wiping away my tears.

"I know I can, can I see how mom is?"

He stares at me, his eyes searching mine as if he's trying to find something. His lips form into a thin line. "If that's what you want." His hand takes mine and we walk into the hospital, he doesn't say anything else to me. He's mad and I understand why, I'd be angry if he was keeping something from me too. He leads me to the surgical floor. "Take a seat, I'm going to find out where Dad is."

I take a seat and wait, there's a strong smell of cleaning solution assaults my nose and I try not to heave, I close my eyes and lean my head back, hoping to ease the nausea that's reared its ugly head.

Footsteps draw my attention and I open my eyes and look toward the sound, Hudson and Harrison are walking toward me. I hate that they both have blank expressions on their faces, I can't brace myself if I don't know what's coming. Harrison pulls me into his arms and I look toward Hudson, he's not looking at me and it hurts, fuck it stings.

"Mia," Harrison begins as he pulls away from me. I tear my gaze away from Hudson and look at Harrison. "Your mom lost so much blood, I spoke to an officer I have on board and he said that from the footage they have of the shooting to when someone found her was almost an hour."

My breath is taken from me, my hands shaking as I wait for him to continue.

"Mia, your mom was in surgery for almost four hours. I'm sorry sweetheart, she didn't make it."

My hand clutches my chest as I try and find a way to breathe but I can't. Dizziness hits me and I sway, my hands reaching out to try and steady myself but I'm already dropping. The darkness coming. I hear yelling but I can't make out what is being said or who's saying it.

MY MOUTH FEELS DRY, LIKE I'VE BEEN EATING DRY crackers. I realize that I'm lying down, what the hell happened? I try and remember what the last thing I remember is? A beeping noise sounds as it hits me, my mom died. I sob, my tears free flowing. Why does Martin have to do this to us? To me? I was nice to him, I never did anything to hurt him and yet all he's done is hurt me. I sob for the loss of my parents, for the loss of my mom, regret as the last thing I said to her was that she didn't give a shit about me and she should leave. I cry for the fact that my mom is never going to be a grandma, she'll never get to see my baby, she'll never see me get married.

I'm not sure how long I cry, the tears slowly start to dry up and I search for the call button, where's Hudson?

"Ms Coleman, I'm Angela, I'm your nurse," a woman says and I open my eyes. "Ms Coleman, you fainted, thankfully your fiancé was there to catch you."

"Where is he?" I ask, my voice croaky.

"He's with his mom, would you like me to get him for you?" the nice nurse asks.

I shake my head. "Is his mom okay?"

The look the nurse gives me doesn't tell me she is. "Can I get you anything?"

I glance at the door, making sure no one is there. "I think I'm pregnant." I whisper, sounding ashamed.

Angela's eyes widen before they shut again. "I did ask your fiancé but he said no."

I lick my lips. "I only found out this morning."

She gives me a reassuring smile. "Okay, well we can check and see how the baby's doing. Would you like me to get Dad while I'm getting the machine?"

I panic. "No, please no."

She touches my head, soothing me as she rubs it. "Okay Ms Coleman, I won't say anything. I'll be back in a few moments and when I return we can lock the door so that no one can come in okay?"

I nod. "Thank you."

She smiles once again and leaves. The minutes tick

away, my heart racing in case Hudson returns while she's gone. I don't want to have to explain anything just now.

Angela returns and she's back with the machine and another woman, they enter the room and immediately lock the door behind them. "Ms Coleman, this is doctor Ojan, she's an OBGYN."

"Hi," I say quietly, my nerves getting the better of me.

"Okay Ms Coleman, can...."

"Mia, please call me Mia," I interrupt, I hate being called Ms Coleman.

Doctor Ojan smiles at me. "Okay, Mia it is. Do you know when your last period was?"

I shake my head. "I don't know." I can't remember, it was before I came home for the summer. "Maybe three months ago?"

"That's okay, we can find out how far along you are. If you could take off your clothes from your waist down."

I do as she says and take off my clothes, closing my eyes I focus on my breathing.

"Okay Mia, this may be a little uncomfortable," she tells me as she inserts something inside of me. "Just a second," she murmurs. "Ah, there we are," she says, triumphantly.

Opening my eyes I look in her direction, she's staring at the screen.

"So from this, it seems as though you're about ten weeks pregnant."

My eyes widen as blood rushes through me and my ears ring. Ten weeks means there's no way it's Martin's baby. Thank God, relief washes through me. I stare at the screen, trying to make it out, but my eyes are blurry as the tears fall freely and I smile unabashedly.

The whoomp whoomp whoomping is music to my ears, the proof that life is there, my baby is there, his or her heart beating away. I choke up at how precious this moment truly is.

"The heartbeat is strong, that's a good sign," Doctor Ojan tells me, "Are you having morning sickness?"

I think about the nausea I've been experiencing and nod. "I'm more fatigued than anything."

She finishes up and I'm free to put on my pants again. "That's perfectly normal for your first trimester." Her beeper goes off and she looks at me. "If you have any worries at all, please see a doctor. I'll leave Angela to explain everything else. I'm sorry to rush off, but I have an emergency. Congratulations, Mia."

I smile genuinely for the first time. "Thank you."

She wheels the machine out of my room, leaving Angela and I in the room alone. "Mia, is it okay if I call you Mia?" she asks softly.

"Of course."

She smiles, "Congratulations."

"Thank you." I can't believe that I actually heard the heartbeat, it made it all that much more real.

"Your fiance told me about what happened to your mom, I am so sorry for your loss."

My eyes fill with tears and I try not to let them fall but they seem to have a mind of their own, they slowly trickle down toward my cheek. "Thank you."

"I know that this is a hard time for you, I also know that you're going through a lot right now so what I may say might not make sense, so I'll give you pamphlets and stuff for you to bring home with you. "You'll see an Obstetrician and your family doctor throughout your pregnancy. You'll receive a letter with dates, so you don't need to worry about that." She hands me some pamphlets, and I stare at the pregnant woman on the front, she's smiling brightly and looks as though she has no cares in the world. That's what I want, to be that carefree while carrying my baby, but I know that's not going to happen, not while Martin is out there.

"Mia, the doctor will be around in a couple of minutes to check up on you, but as we now know that you're pregnant, he'll probably let you go, the shock of losing your mom in such a horrific way is most probably why you fainted. Again, I'm extremely sorry for your loss."

"Thank you, for everything," I tell her and watch as she walks out the door, I quickly fold the pamphlets up that she gave me and put them into my pocket, grateful that I wore pants that have them.

I hope the doctor comes soon, I really want to leave and check on Hudson, Angela gave me the impression that things with his mom had changed. That's not good, he was so positive that she was going to be okay, she would be in a lot of pain but she was fine. What changed? Were the doctors wrong?

The door opens and in walks Hudson, as soon as I see him it's like a damn breaks inside of me, my body bucking as I sob. His arms are around me within seconds.

"I'm sorry, Princess. I'm so fucking sorry," he says.

My arms go around his neck and I sob into his chest. "It...Wasn't...Your...Fault," I tell him through my wails, all the while he holds me tightly.

He lifts me off the bed, sits down on it, and places me onto his lap, it's something he always does when he wants to get closer to me. He holds me until my tears dry once again. "Is your mom okay?" I ask as soon as I'm able to talk properly.

"She has a pulmonary embolism, they have given her the drugs to help reduce it. But she's okay, they caught it early, it could have been a lot worse," his voice cracking, it's been one hell of a day, we're all feeling it.

"I'm glad they caught it early. Was it due to the surgery?"

He pulls me closer, placing a kiss against my head. "We're not sure, Princess, it may not be, it could be from the shot, or she may have had one beforehand. They can't be certain, but it's been found and they're working on getting rid of it."

I turn so that I can see him. "How are you?" It must have been hard learning that his mom was shot not to mention that she was in surgery.

His eyebrows raise as his eyes widen. "Me? Princess, you've just lost your mom and you're asking me how I'm doing?"

I nod. "Yes, I'm asking you how you're doing. Your mom was shot, she had surgery Hudson, that's a big deal. Not to mention you saw me faint."

His eyes shutter close, pain etched on his face. "Fuck, I'm begging you, please don't do that again."

I giggle. "It's not like I intended to do it."

He hugs me tightly. "I know you didn't. God, it was awful. I'll probably have nightmares for the rest of my life."

"I'm sorry," I tell him, placing a kiss against his lips. "How's your dad? He must be taking this pretty hard." Having his ex-wife as well as his current wife shot within hours of each other.

"He's putting on a brave face, but I know it's killing him inside. As much as he and your mom argued toward the end, mainly about me. My dad loved her, you were right what you said, my dad gave her everything she wanted, he was happiest with her and now she's gone."

"I don't know what happened to my mom, but she loved your dad, she really did. When she spoke about him, it was with pure happiness. When Lacey and I came to their house in Hidden Hills, I can honestly say that I had never seen my mom as happy as I did then. Your dad was the best thing that happened to her and I'm glad that she had that love. That she had someone who worshiped her as your dad did. I think everyone deserves to feel that love once in their life."

He nods. "I'm going to get him Mia, and I'm going to make sure that he's out of our lives for good."

I wish I could believe that, I really do but this has been going on for too long now. "He's taken the only blood family I had left. He's taken so much from me Hudson. So fucking much. I don't understand why I'm the one being punished?"

"I want to take this hurt away from you, Baby. I wish I could tell you that I'll have him tomorrow but the truth is, I don't know where he is and until I do, I'm chasing a fucking ghost. The man has hurt you in ways that I will never understand but feel every night we go to bed because every night you have a nightmare and I try and comfort you, you flinch. That's on him. The man has killed your best friend, a woman I grew close to, even though it was only for a couple of weeks, I feel that because she was your girl. He also killed your mom, my dad's wife and I'll feel that pain too because you both feel it deeply. He killed my men, he's killed my men's wives. He's gone after my mom. I feel these things, and I'm burying them, Baby, as I'm biding my time, I'm going to get him, it may not be tomorrow, or next week, but one day I'm going to get him and that anger I feel is going to come out and he's going to feel every single thing."

Oh my God. "Hudson," I whisper, unable to say anything else. I wrap my arms around him, offering the support that he offers me without question.

"Princess, I know that the longer he's out there the

more you're going to worry but I'm doing everything I can to find him. My men are working tirelessly to find him. I see the disappointment in your eyes every time I come home and I haven't found him. I see it all, including the fact that you're hiding something from me."

I sigh, not releasing him. "I know I am and I promise Hudson, I'll tell you, but not here."

He pulls me away from him, his hands moving to my face, he's silent as his eyes searches mine. "Okay Princess, tonight it's just you and me."

I nod, that sounds good. "Okay Hudson, just me and you."

"Good, I'm going to see if I can find the doctor and see if I can bring you home."

I nod. "That'll be good, I want to get out of here, but I want to see your mom and dad first." I need to make sure that they're okay. Let his dad know that he's not alone, I'm grieving with him too.

THREE

Hudson

THE DOCTOR HAS FINALLY COME by to see Mia, he's allowed her to go home, which has made me less fucking anxious. I thought that she'd be here for the night and I know what these hospitals are like with visitors, I wouldn't be able to stay here with her which would give Martin easy access to her.

She grips my arm tightly, as we walk toward my mom, she doesn't look as grey as she had. She'll be the death of me, I swear her fainting took years off my life. I'm grateful that I managed to catch her, her head was inches from the floor.

"Hudson, are you okay? You're quiet?" she asks me softly.

I'm so surprised by her, she's more worried about me than anything. Her mom's just died and yet she's focused on checking on my parents. "Yeah, Princess,"

"Mmhmm."

"What's mmhmm about?"

"Mmhmm is mmhmm, you're full of shit. You're never this quiet."

I stop her in her tracks. "Mia, I'm fine, there's nothing wrong, I am usually this quiet."

She gives me a smile. "You may be quiet, but never with me. Let's go see your parents and then we can go home." She takes my hand and starts walking again.

"Mia…"

She shakes her head. "I understand, we're all going through a lot and we're still getting to know each other. Your silence is your way of sorting everything out. I guess we're similar in that sense."

"Yeah baby, we are. I'm fucking tired, let's get this over and done with and go home."

She rolls her eyes at me. "Over and done with? Damn, don't you have a way with words?"

I know this is just her putting on a brave face, she hates feeling the hurt and the pain. She buries it until she has to deal with it and then when she does, she feels it ten times worse. The night of Lacey's funeral, I found Mia in the bathroom of our hotel room, her knees curled into her body as she lay on the floor sobbing. The pain pouring out of her with every breath she took. I know that she's cried for her mom, but that's all she'll allow herself for now, until the time comes when she has to grieve. Then I'll be there to make sure she doesn't break.

I open the door to Mom's room and immediately Mom's head turns to face us. As soon as she sees Mia she holds out her arms and Mia doesn't hesitate to walk into them, being careful as she wraps her arms around my mom.

"We're not staying long. You need to rest and so does Mia, she wanted to check in on you. Make sure you're okay."

Mom tsks. "Darling girl I'm okay. It'll take more than a

bullet to stop me. I'm sorry about your mom, if you ever need anything all you have to do is ask."

"Thank you, Marline. I'm glad you're okay."

"Mom, have you seen Dad? Mia wants to check on him before we leave too."

She shakes her head, "No, I haven't. He left when you went back to Mia. He's not been back since."

I step outside her room and call him, he answers straight away. "Where are you?"

"I'm outside, is Mia okay?"

"Yeah, she can't wait to get home. She wanted to check on you and Mom, she's with Mom now."

"I'm fine, she doesn't need to check up on me."

I laugh. "Yeah, you know Mia, that's not going to work."

He sighs. "Fuck, okay, meet me outside when you're finished."

I roll my eyes, he's being a fucking pussy not wanting to be around Mom. "We'll be down in a few minutes." I end the call and walk back inside Mom's room.

"Did you find your father?" Mom asks.

"Yeah, he's waiting outside for us."

Mom laughs. "Yeah, I think your father is a bit jittery around me. I don't understand why, it's not like I was the one to betray him. I was faithful in our marriage."

Christ. "Now isn't the time Mom."

She shrugs. "It's the truth, the man is a coward. He doesn't care about anyone but himself."

I glance at Mia, she's looking down at her hands, her lips pulled into a thin line. She's trying her best to keep quiet. "Mom, now isn't the damn time," I say through gritted teeth.

Mom realizes what she's said and looks sheepishly at Mia, "Sorry."

Mia shrugs, "No need to apologize."

"Come on, we'd better go and find Dad. Don't want him to have something to complain about." I reach out and take Mia's hand. "Mom, I'll stop by tomorrow, try not to annoy any of the nursing staff."

She looks insulted. "I wouldn't dare, I'll be the best patient they'll ever have."

"Of course you will be."

"Bye, Marline." Mia says softly and I think she's upset about what Mom was saying but she won't say anything. She's just not like that. As soon as we're out of Mom's room she asks me about Dad. "Is he okay?"

No he isn't, I can tell by his voice and the way he's acting. He's distracted, his mind is elsewhere. "I'd say he's as okay as you are."

She makes a weird noise in the back of her throat. "That good huh?"

"You'll both get there, Princess."

She stops and turns to face me. "I know we will. You'll get us there, just like you did when Lacey died and after he raped me."

Fuck me. "Mia…" my voice cracks, what the fuck is this girl doing to me? "You're incredible, Princess, there's no other way to describe you."

She presses her lips together. "I'm not going to cry." Her nostrils flare as she tries not to cry. "I love you. When we get home, we'll talk, okay?"

"Sounds ominous. Love you too though, Princess, that's never going to change." I pull her toward me, her head resting against my shoulder. "Let's go get Dad."

Walking outside, Dad's waiting for us, and just like Mom he opens his arms and Mia willingly walks into them, they whisper to one another, whatever Mia says to Dad has his eyes closed in pain. They pull away from each other, and Mia wipes tears from her eyes as she walks back toward me, her arms sliding around my waist.

"I'll leave you two alone tonight, I'll swing by tomorrow." That's his way of saying he wants his space. I can't even begin to imagine what he's going through, I'd lose my shit if Mia died, I'd go on a rampage, I'd kill everyone in sight. I wouldn't give a shit who I took down. Dad's being calm and I'm waiting until his anger hits, because that's when the shit's going to hit the fan.

We say our goodbyes and Mia and I go back to the car, she's gone quiet again and I know she's thinking about whatever Dad said to her. Mia and her mom had a rough end to their relationship, and I'm partly responsible, if I hadn't met Mia again, none of this would have happened but at the same time, I wouldn't change it all, she's fucking amazing.

The drive to our house is quiet and I'm starting to get on edge, I'm wondering what Mia wants to talk about. Whatever has happened, it sure as fuck has me on edge. I've had every scenario running through my mind, and yet I can't think of anything that could have happened. If it has to do with Martin, I'll lose the damn plot. She's staring out the window, the entire journey, her mind elsewhere.

"I'm going to get changed, I won't be long," she says as I open the door, she pushes past me and rushes to our bedroom. I leave her be, knowing that she won't say anything, not just yet. Let her come to me, it'll be the best way for her to open up to me. Walking into the kitchen, I grab a beer and wait for Mia in the sitting room.

She walks into the sitting room, dressed in my t-shirt, it's hanging off her. She sits on the sofa that's opposite me, I see that she's not wearing panties and my mind instantly transports back to the day I found her on that filthy fucking mattress. "So," she begins, and I look at her. "I haven't been feeling well lately."

I frown, "What?"

She shrugs, "I've been more tired than usual, I've been getting heartburn, and I've been feeling nauseous."

"Okay?" I'm still confused, why didn't she tell me.

"I thought it was stress, everything that I'd been through, I presumed it was that." She sounds so worried.

"Mia, tell me what's going on?"

"I realized that I was late, or that I couldn't remember the last time I had one."

"Mia, Princess, you're going to have to break it down for me."

"Hudson, I bought a pregnancy test and I took it this morning." A tear slowly slides down her face, I follow it as it drops to her cheek and onto her lip.

My breath leaves me in a whoosh, my eyes widen as I realize just what she's saying. "Mia, are you pregnant?"

She nods. "Yes, I'm pregnant."

I blink. "Why didn't you tell me?"

She glances at her hands, wringing them together. "Because I wasn't sure who the father was." More tears fall from her, I don't watch them this time, instead I get up off the sofa and walk over to her. Crouching down in front of her, I wipe the tears away. "I didn't want to tell you, I didn't want you to know."

"That it could be his?" She nods, the tears falling faster. "Princess, do you think I give a shit? You're mine and that means any baby you have is mine too."

She sobs. "I didn't know if I could raise his baby. I didn't know if I would be strong enough." She wipes her tears and looks at me. "I wasn't sure if I could overlook what he did to me and see the beautifulness of the baby." She shakes her head. "I was scared." She confesses quietly

"Whatever you want to do, I'm behind you every step of the way." I say without hesitation.

She nods. "I don't think I could get rid of the baby."

I guess it's something that she has to decide for herself. "What about when you fainted? Are you both okay?"

She reaches her hand out and her fingers intertwine with mine. "Yes, we're both fine."

I bring her hands to my lips and kiss them. "Whatever happens, we'll get through it. I meant what I said princess, if it's his, I don't give a shit, your kid, is mine too." I'll make sure that Martin has no fucking idea that Mia's pregnant, he'll never get to see my child. Ever.

Her lips part, and her tears are soaking her eyelashes but she smiles so brightly. "It's not his Hudson," she whispers and it's like a punch in the gut, the wind is taken from me. "I love you, I love that you would have raised this baby with me if it wasn't yours. But it is."

"What?" I need to hear her say those words again.

She squeezes my hand. "It's not his baby, it's yours."

Fuck.

"We're having a baby," she tells me her grin from ear to ear.

"Seriously?" She nods. "How do you know?" I have no idea about this shit.

"They did a scan at the hospital, we're ten weeks." That smile just gets wider and wider.

Ten weeks? "Wait… ten weeks?" Her eyes narrow but she nods. "So the first night." I can't help but grin.

She rolls her eyes. "I didn't say that."

"But?" I can't help but smirk.

She closes her eyes and shakes her head. "Fine, you got me pregnant in the first week."

I kiss her lips. "The first week," I murmur.

She pushes me away. "I told you to put on a damn condom."

"You loved it," I quip.

She rolls her eyes at me again. "That may be so. I still can't wrap my head around this. We're pregnant."

"We're pregnant," I echo her words. "I can't believe I'm going to be a dad." I lift her off the sofa and her legs go around my waist, her arms going around my neck.

"I'm sorry I never told you right away, I was scared." She leans her head on my shoulder.

I kiss her softly, "Princess, don't apologize." I understand why she never said anything. She was scared, she's been through a lot, and Martin has put her through hell.

"I'm still scared though, Hudson."

My gut tightens at her words, I know why she is and I hate that I can't fucking do anything about it. "I'm going to get him Mia, he won't hurt you, he won't hurt our baby."

She nods. "What if he finds out about the baby? What if he thinks it's his?"

I have no answer, because I honestly don't know what he'll do. "You're safe, Mia that I can promise you." My hands squeeze her ass cheeks. "Now isn't the time to think about him. It's time to celebrate." Her head lifts off my shoulder, her green eyes so bright, so full of happiness. My lips descend on hers, my tongue sweeping into her mouth and dominating hers.

I undo my pants so that my cock is free, turning to Mia, I lift her so that she's straddling me, it takes ages before she lowers herself completely down on my dick, her hands intertwine with mine and she leans forward and places a kiss on my lips. "Love you," she whispers.

"Princess, I fucking love you. I'd go to hell and back for you. But baby, you've got to move." I thrust inside of her, pushing myself deeper than I've been before. Mia throws her head back and cries out with pleasure. My hands grip her hips and I lift her so that only the head of my dick is inside of her warm, wet pussy and push back into her.

"Fuck!" She cries out and I do it again, her hands releasing mine, going to my chest. I do it again, pulling out a little bit more and thrusting all the way inside of her again. "Yes," she whispers, her fingers digging into my skin.

I'm getting close, I lift her off me and place her on her back. Her legs automatically open for me, and I thrust back inside of her. Her hands go to my shoulders and she begins to fuck me just as I do her, we're in sync. The sounds of our ragged breathing, along with our bodies hitting off one another is all that can be heard.

She grinds down on my cock as she comes, the walls of her pussy contracting against my dick, pulling my cum from me. "Mia." I growl as I thrust, once, twice, three times inside of her, trying to get as far inside of her as I can.

"Fuck, I love you." I breathe as I place a kiss against her lips, pulling out of her and collapsing beside her.

We lie on the sofa in silence, both of us trying to regain our breath.

"Do you think your dad's okay?" She asks me after a few moments in silence.

"He will be," I tell her, I have something for him to do, it'll help him take his mind off things as well as release some of that anger he has.

She turns so she's lying on her side, her smile is sad as is the look in her eyes. "A part of me wants to tell him about the baby, but I know that right now, we all need to focus on finding Martin and both he and I need to grieve, once we have, then we can tell him."

She always manages to say something that I wouldn't expect. "Yeah Princess, I think that's a good idea. Dad needs to come to terms with what's happened, knowing my dad, he's probably kicking himself for pushing her away."

Tears shine in her eyes. "She deserved it, the way she was acting…" she trails off shaking her head. "I wish she'd have known how much we really did love her."

I pull her into my arms. "She did, trust me baby, she knew." That I have no doubts about, both of them loved her unconditionally, yes, they were mad, but that didn't change how they felt. Tina would have known that.

"I hope that she's with dad. I know they didn't love each other romantically, but they did love each other. I want them to look after each other now." The tears slowly fall down her face, "What am I going to do? They're both gone."

"They're not completely gone, Princess. They're still in your heart." Great I sound like a damn sap. "You have the memories you made with them, they're never going to go."

She nods, the tears falling thicker and faster, I reach over and wipe them away. "I'm alone," she whispers.

She's fucking gutting me, she's not even twenty yet and both her parents are dead, one because of this fucking war that I'm in. She was an innocent, she didn't deserve to die. "You're not alone, you have me." My hand touches her stomach. "You have us both."

She gives me a watery smile. "I do."

My cell phone rings and her body stills under my hand. Every time that thing fucking rings, it brings bad news, what the hell has happened now.

FOUR

Mia

FEAR, that's all I feel whenever his cell rings. "Don't answer it." I can't deal with anything else today, we've all been through enough.

"I have to," he tells me, placing a chaste kiss to my lips. He climbs out of the bed, and reaches for his pants that are on the ground. "It could be the hospital."

Shit, I've been so caught up in myself and losing mom and the baby that I completely forgot about Marline. I'm such a bitch.

"It's one of the men," he tells me and answers the phone, "Rory, talk to me." He walks out of the bedroom, completely naked.

I reach for my phone, I need to call Sarah. I put Facetiming calling and wait. Pulling Hudson's t-shirt off the floor, I quickly throw it over my head and sit up. She doesn't make me wait long. "Mia." Her eyes are watery, she's heard.

"Hey you," I say softly and her tears slowly fall. "How's Allie?"

She wipes away the tears. "She's fine, more importantly how are you? Hudson told me what happened."

I shrug, right now, I'm numb. I've been numb since I've found out. Hudson has made me happy, hell having sex made me feel alive but I'm back to where I was, feeling numb. "I'm okay."

She glares at me. "You're full of shit."

I nod. "Yeah, I am. I don't know what to do, what am I supposed to do? Sarah, the fucker is still out there, he's still hurting people. But what I don't understand is why he had to kill Lacey and mom?" They had nothing to do with this, so why on earth did they have to die? What did I, or they, do to him to make him want to kill them? To make me hurt so deeply?

She shakes her head. "Mia, I have no idea what goes through his damn head. I don't *want* to see what goes through it either."

I can just imagine the evil that runs through it. "Let's not talk about this anymore," I tell her, as I wipe away my tears.

"Hey Mia, I'm really sorry about your mom." Frankie says, coming into view, as he stands behind Sarah."

"Thanks." I give him a sad smile, really hoping he'll leave it as that.

"If you need anything, don't hesitate to give me a call."

"Thank you," I reply and watch as Sarah rolls her eyes.

We stay here in silence, as Frankie just stands behind Sarah. I'm dying to tell Sarah about the pregnancy but I know that I can't, not yet. I haven't told her everything about what happened with Martin. She's going to be so hurt that I've not confided in her about any of this.

"Frankie, go away, we're talking," Sarah tells him as she pushes him away.

He smirks, "See you later Mia."

I wave at him. "Bye."

Sarah laughs, "God, he's so weird. He's got a crush on you."

I give her a *get real* look, "Yeah, right."

She continues to laugh. "I swear to you, Mia, he's got the biggest crush on you, it's why he was pissed at Lacey's funeral when he found out you and Hudson were engaged."

"Where's Jagger?" I ask changing the subject.

"He's working." The fear in her voice is clear to hear.

"He'll be okay." Even as I say the words, I don't believe them. Martin doesn't give a shit who he hurts and he certainly wouldn't hesitate in hurting Jagger.

"I'm hoping so, Mia. We've finally got somewhere where we're both happy."

I smile, this time it's a genuine one. "You love him and he loves you."

"I know, he's promised me that he'll never hurt me again." She sighs and I know there's something she's not saying. I wait, letting the silence fill us. "I'm worried that he'll go back to Carina."

"Never," I say vehemently. "That was over before he found out about Allie. Trust me Sarah, Carina is someone you don't have to worry about. Jagger loves you."

She rubs her hands over her arms, "That's what he said too."

"I wouldn't lie to you, Sarah, if I thought there was even the slightest chance about it, I'd tell you," I promise her.

Relief shines through in her eyes. "Yeah, you're right." She shakes her head, "God, when did this get about me? I'm sorry."

"Don't apologize, I was glad of the reprieve."

Allie cries in the background. "I'm sorry Mia, I'm

going to have to go, that's her just waking up. She'll be hungry."

"Don't apologize, I'll talk to you later. Bye, Sarah."

She blows me a kiss. "Bye, Mia." She ends the call.

I sit here, and search through my pictures. I realize as I flick through them that there aren't that many of Hudson and I. I have loads of Lacey and I, even of mom and I. I smile when I see the picture of Lacey and I, we were in the car on our way to Hidden Hills, we'd just pulled over to get something to eat. We're both making weird faces. God, I miss her so much. She didn't deserve to die, she was the sweetest girl ever, she never upset anyone. For Martin to be the one to kill her hurts, she really liked him and he ended her life.

The tears fall down my face and I let them. I come across a picture of mom, Lacey and I, it was the night that Hudson and I reunited, Mom and Harrison's marriage celebration. After Lacey and I were dressed, Mom came into the room and we took a picture of the three of us. Looking at this picture, I see the woman that was so in love, so beyond happy that her smile was infectious. I carry on scrolling, loving just how many pictures I have of the two women that had the greatest impact on my life. I come across a picture of Mom and Harrison, I don't remember taking it, mom is in Harrison's arms, her head tilted back to look at him, they both have matching smiles, and the look of love they have reminds me of the look that Hudson has when he looks at me.

The bed dips and I glance to my left to see Hudson sitting beside me. I lean my head against his shoulder. "Everything okay?"

He kisses my head. "Yeah, Princess, just Dad checking in to see how you are."

I lift my phone and show him the screen.

"When you see that, you can't deny that they really loved each other."

"No, you can't. I can't think about losing you, just the thought makes my heart hurt. I can't imagine what your father's going through right now."

"I lost you, fuck, I fell apart on the inside. I'm not going to lie, Princess, I am nothing without you, that's for fucking sure. I couldn't sleep, I couldn't fucking eat. I was in limbo, I had no idea if you were alive, or if he had killed you. The thought of you dying," he shakes his head, his Adam's apple bobbing up and down as he swallows hard. "So, Princess, I get a fifth of what my dad's feeling, right now he's dealing with it. There's going to come a time when he's going to let the darkness take over."

I inhale sharply, lifting my head so that I'm looking at him. "What can we do?"

The look on Hudson's face says it all, nothing. "Baby, we let that darkness take over, but we make sure it doesn't consume him. If we do, we may as well bury him with your mom. He's going to want revenge, the thing is, we're all looking for revenge on the same man, there's three of us that he's hurt our women, two where he's actually killed, but Mia, what he did to you…" He turns his head away from me, "I promised you that I'd get him, that I'd end him. I intend to keep my promise, even if it's having two men that I care about not being able to exact revenge."

"Why?" I ask tentatively, unsure of what his answers going to be. "Why wouldn't you let them do it?"

"Mia, you are mine. What he did to you no woman should ever go through. He did that to you so that he could get revenge on me for some shit I had no idea even happened. He took you, even after everything I had done for him, he raped you knowing that it would break you, and in turn gut me. The man did it thinking that he'd bury me."

"But he didn't, none of those things are true."

Hudson looks at me, his deep brown eyes so dark, so full of hate. "I'm glad that fucker never broke you Mia, that he didn't bury me but fuck, hearing you say what he did to you. It gutted me, deeper than anything could ever gut me."

I gasp at his words, I didn't know he felt that way.

"Mia, I love you, I'm the one that's supposed to protect you and knowing that I couldn't, hurts, knowing that he did that to you along with killing your best friend in front of you is on me…"

"No, it's not!" I cut him off, not believing the words that are coming out of his mouth right now. "If it were the other way around, would you think it was my fault?"

"No, that makes no sense."

I stare at him. "Well I love you, I'm supposed to protect you…" I mimic the words he's just said to me.

"It's different."

I frown. "How is it different? Because I'm a woman and you're a man? Do you not think that I can protect you? That I'm not capable of doing so?"

"Yes, Mia, you are a woman. You deserve to be cherished, protected, loved. No one has the right to hurt you. No one has the right to hurt what's mine."

"If I'm yours then you are mine!"

"Obviously," he replies as though I'm stupid.

"So, why can't I want to protect you? Why can't I want to make sure nothing hurts you? Why can't I make sure that the man I love is safe? Why, Hudson?" The tears are close again, I'm so sick and tired of crying.

"Mia…"

I shake my head. "It's double standards Hudson, it's

not fair, I have just as much rights to protect you as you do me. This relationship is fifty-fifty and that means what we do, we do together. We're a partnership. God, we're going to get married. You need to realize that I want the best for you."

He pulls me toward him. "You're one of a kind. You're right, we're in a partnership, this relationship is even. So you protect me as much as I protect you."

Relief washes through me. "Good."

"You're a passionate little thing."

I groan. "I won't be little for much longer. What if I'm having a boy? I'll be as big as a house, especially if he takes after his dad."

"We don't have girls," he tells me and I laugh at how serious he looks. "Mia it's not funny. The life we lead, the business we have, it's why we only have boys."

I laugh. "I'm sorry, Hudson, I don't have that power over what gender our baby is going to be. Although, I would be happy with either sex." I give him a pointed look, kind of mad that he's wanting a boy, what's going to happen if we have a girl? Is he not going to want her?

"I know that, I'm just not sure I have the strength to be a father for a girl, nor do I have the ammunition to fight off all the men that are going to be after her if she looks like you."

"Flattery will get you everywhere. Look, Hudson, how about we cross that path when we reach it? There's no point in stressing about it right now."

He smiles, his hands caressing my stomach. He pushes me back so that I'm lying flat on my back, lifting the t-shirt over my head, he kisses my stomach. "God, you've made me the happiest man ever." He throws the t-shirt to the floor.

I smile. "Well that's good, seeing as you've made me

the happiest I've ever been. It's only fair that I reciprocate it."

"I never thought I'd meet someone like you. With the way my parents were, and the fact that I'm the most powerful man in California, I thought that I too would have to marry just for an heir."

"We're not even married and now you have an heir on the way." I smile. "Now is the time to run." My laughter turns into a full blown cackle as I take in his narrowed eyes.

He leans over me, his entire body, over mine. His dick thick and erect once again, it's nudging at my pussy where my legs are closed. "I'm not going anywhere. I've told you from the get-go, that you're mine and I mean it." His lips descend on mine, the kiss is hard and fast. He pulls back. "Do you want out?" He raises his eyebrows at me.

I grab his face with both of my hands and kiss him, my tongue sweeping into his mouth, my legs parting allowing him access to my pussy. As soon as his dick touches my opening, he takes over the kiss, his hands going to my thighs, he lifts my legs and enters me in one swift movement.

My back arches as my mouth opens in shock, as he fills me, I feel complete with him inside of me. His kiss is intoxicating, it's as though our mouths are fused together, I don't want to stop, this is heaven, this is where I belong, with him, with the man I love. I lose myself in the bliss, loving every thrust, every groan that comes from Hudson. I know that without him, my life wouldn't be complete.

"Baby, come back to me." He whispers in my ear as he thrusts inside me again.

"I'm here." I moan, "I'm with you, always," I tell him honestly.

"Good," he grunts as he picks up his pace. "You

close?" he growls, and hearing that deep noise at the back of his throat makes me shiver. "Yeah, Princess, you're close."

He lifts my thighs higher and I do the only thing I can think of, I wrap my legs around his neck. As soon as he thrusts into me I moan loudly, he's hitting the right spot, it feels so good. "Oh God," I cry out as his finger goes to my clit. "Hudson," I whimper, it's too much.

"Give it to me, Princess," he groans and I know what he wants, he wants me to submit to the pleasure, give him everything. So I do, I let the pleasure take over, tingles start to spread throughout my body and I detonate against his dick. He follows right behind me, kissing me as he fills my pussy with his cum.

"God, you're a machine," I tell him after I manage to recover.

His laughter sends shivers down my spine. God, I love hearing that. "Mia, I'm the happiest man in the world, my fiancée is fucking gorgeous and she's carrying my child. If you think I'm not going to fuck you just because you're pregnant, you're sadly mistaken."

I smirk. "Oh you're one of those."

"One of what?" he asks through clenched teeth.

"Those men that love it when their women are pregnant."

He smiles. "Yeah, I am. We're going to have loads of children."

I shake my head. "How about we have one and go from there?"

"Fine," he grumbles and I laugh, he's acting like a child.

I reach for the sheets and pull them up over me. I didn't realize how tired I was until just now, my eyes heavy and I cover my mouth as a yawn breaks through.

"Take a nap, Princess, I've a few calls to make and then we'll have some dinner?"

I yawn again. "Sounds good." I pucker my lips and he laughs, I'm too lazy to move and kiss him. He places a chaste kiss against my lips and gets off the bed. I sink into the bed further and close my eyes. It doesn't take long for sleep to come.

FIVE

Hudson
———

BY THE TIME I'm closing the door, Mia's already asleep. I think I may have pushed her too hard. She's been through the ringer today and my selfish ass has had her twice. I can't help myself when I'm around her, she's beautiful and seeing her naked pushes me over the edge. When I came back in the bedroom after talking to dad and found her crying, I did the only thing I could, I cheered her up. I hate seeing her cry, and I have no idea how I'm supposed to help her through this grief other than be with her.

My cell rings as I walk into the kitchen, looking at the screen I see it's my dad again. "Hey, everything okay?"

"Yeah, so I'm with Rory and his brother, Cormac, could you not find anyone more Irish?"

I laugh, the Callahan brothers are as Irish as you can get, and they're the perfect stereotype. Red hair, freckles, catholic, and a thick accent. "Probably, what's up?"

"I'm sitting outside of Noreen's house. Fuck Hudson, Rory's right. Martin's a lying son of a bitch. She's alive as is his father."

I don't correct him on the fact that he's his father, and leave it be. "What are you going to do?"

"I'm going to show that fucker what it's like to lose someone you care about. He's hidden them for a reason, he cares about them. It's time to take from him, just as he took from me, as he took from Mia. It's time for revenge." His voice dark and full of anger, this is the man I grew up with, he's reverting back to the man he was.

"Call if you need me," I tell him and he doesn't reply, I get dead air. He's focused on what he's about to do. This is going to cause mayhem and I'm looking forward to seeing that fucker reel with the impact of losing his parents, he's going to feel exactly what Mia's feeling right now.

I make myself a whiskey, I need to call Jagger and find out if he has a lead on Johnson, if not, the best way to make him come out is to take his ex-wife. Walking into my office, I take a seat, and hit dial for Jagger's number. I take a sip of whiskey, loving the burn as it goes down my throat.

"Boss," he answers.

"Jag, how are you with getting what I've asked."

He laughs. "Boss, you called at just the right time. The fucker has been hiding but we've finally found him. Bringing him in now."

I smile, everything is falling into place. "Good."

"Boss, how is your mom and Tina?"

Shit, I forgot that my men don't know what's happened. "Mom's good. She came out of surgery and her usual self. Tina, didn't make it."

"Fuck." That one word resonates with me. It's the only way to describe it. "How's Mia and your dad?"

"About as well as you'd think. Mia's asleep and Dad's out doing something."

He laughs. "I know what that means, I'll call you when we're situated."

"Good, call if you need me." I end the call, I hate not being in the action but right now, Mia needs me more than anything.

Throwing my phone onto my desk I boot up my laptop, Dad told me earlier that the man he hired to delve into how Mia was taken had sent me a file. Loading up my emails, I see the email Dad was talking about. It's from a Bounty Hunter that I know, Cody Haines. Why has he gone to Cody? I read the email, and understand why dad went to him.

Hudson,

Martin came to me about two months ago, asking me for listening devices and trackers. He told me that you had someone on your tail and wanted to reciprocate the favor. Had I known what he really intended on using it for, I would never have given him the devices.

He planted the tracker and listening device in Mia's phone, I've tracked it as I too have a tracking chip inside, in case it got into the wrong hands. Hudson, it's still there, he's still listening. Also, I have an exact location on where he last used the device that was less than twenty four hours ago. I've attached a map that pinpoints his location.

I'd love nothing more than to help you bring down this bastard but I'm on a skip at the moment in Maryland. Call me if you need me.

All the best,
 Cody.

. . .

FUCK, FUCK, FUCK. I'M UP OFF MY CHAIR AND STALKING toward our bedroom, it's time to get Mia a new phone. Opening the bedroom door, I spy her phone on the bed. I know that I can't throw it away, not yet at least. I need to move her pictures and shit over to her new one and then I'm going to use this as a way to make Martin pay. He's obviously still keeping tabs on her, Coby said that he last used the listening device less than twenty four hours ago. We're finally, fucking finally, finding the mistakes he's making. He's about to lose everything he has, no more leverage, no more comforts, he's going to be fucked.

I go through her images and make sure they're all saved to her memory card, not wanting her to lose any on the changeover. I send a text to Aaron, asking him to get Mia a new phone, needing to get this shit out of her hands as soon as possible. Once she wakes, I'm going to have to explain to her why I'm taking her cell away from her.

I leave the bedroom, wanting her to sleep a bit longer. I'm still shocked that she's pregnant, when she told me and that she was scared that it was Martin's my heart dropped to my stomach, but I meant what I said to her, even if it was his, I'd still consider it my own because there is no way on this fucking earth that bastard was ever going to even lay eyes on Mia again. I know that as soon as my men find out Mia's pregnant they're going to come to the conclusion that it could be his, my men gossip like fucking old women in a hair salon and there's no way they haven't found out what that fucker did to Mia.

Aaron replies to me saying he's on his way to get one now, he'll drop it by the house once it's been purchased. I don't ask him where he's getting it from or what cell he's getting. I know my man, he'll get the best one available to him at the time. It's why I've asked him to get it, he'll know what to get and won't have to ask me what the hell he needs to buy.

I'm waiting on Dad to call back, it's been at least thirty minutes, and I've never known it to take that long to off someone. I know he won't have got cold feet, but I am wondering if he's gone overboard and has ended up torturing them. I've seen my dad go crazy as fuck, once before, he ended up decapitating them, as well as slaughtering their entire family. I was eleven when I witnessed it and it's why I've sworn that I'll always protect innocent women and children. If women fuck up, they'll pay the price, I'm not that much of a martyr.

My cell rings and I see that it's Jagger. I answer it immediately. "He there?"

"Yes boss, what do you want me to do with him?"

"Hold him there, I'm waiting on Aaron to arrive and I'll be there." I'm not sure yet if I'll bring both Aaron and Mia along or leave him here to watch her. "Has he said anything?"

"Not yet." There's a slight mocking in his tone, and I'm curious as to what they've done to him.

"I'll be there shortly." I end the call and walk back to the office and grab my whiskey. I down it in one swallow, I hate fucking waiting and dad's taking his time. I wonder if they're having a trip down memory lane, talking about how fucked up their son is? It's hard to think that asshole's my brother, the trust I had in him was misplaced, had I known what he was that trust wouldn't have been there. I'd have been suspicious of him from the get-go, I'd have been wary of his motives, always wondering what angle he would have been playing. I'd have known that he was passed over for the title of Boss, I'd have known that it would hurt him and I'd have known that he'd want revenge, I'd have been prepared for what was to come. I would have been one step ahead. Whereas now, I'm at least three moves behind and finally gaining ground. It's too late, way fucking too late.

I hear a noise in the bedroom, followed by footsteps, Mia's awake. I follow the noise, just as she comes out of the bathroom. "You have a good sleep?"

Her arms reach above her head as she stretches. "Yes, but it wasn't long enough." She yawns, her hand covering her mouth as she does.

"We've got to go out, but once we return, you can sleep all night." I promise her.

Her eyebrows raise, "All night?"

I smirk knowing what she's getting at. I hold my hands up, "I'll leave you be…" She smiles. "For this evening," I finish and she shakes her head but that smile is still present on her face. "I'll have Aaron stop for some food on the way."

She walks to the wardrobe and starts getting dressed. "Where are we going?"

I sit at the edge of the bed and watch as she pulls on her dress. "I have a bit of business to attend to, I had debated leaving you here with Aaron but I can't part with you, I can't guarantee your safety with anyone but me."

She walks over to me, her arms going around my neck. "I'm not going to argue with you, I know that you have my best interests at heart, if you say it's for the best I'll go along with it," she tells me placing a kiss against my lips. "Just don't lie to me," she begs.

"I won't," I promise her. "I won't lie to you. Sometimes I can't tell you about my business and that's not because I don't trust you. It's because it's to do with my men. I came to realize something this morning, I had a Fed on my back, the man was on me constantly, I couldn't piss without the asshole being there. Then all of a sudden he's gone and

Martin's gone crazy. It didn't make sense. That's where we're heading, we're going to find out what the Fed knows."

She sits down beside me, her hand clasping mine. "Hudson, this is a Federal agent, you can't kidnap him. You'll go to prison."

I smile, she's so fucking innocent. She doesn't understand. "Mia, I'm not going to go to prison, that I can assure you. That fucking Fed is crooked, there's no way he's going to report that he's been taken, that's if I let him go."

She sighs. "God, Hudson, if he goes missing they're going to look at you. You'll be the first person they look at."

"Princess, trust me, I've been doing this a long time, I know how to make things look like an accident or a suicide. There's no way it'll trace back to me."

"I trust you," she replies instantly.

"Good, now, there's one more thing that I need to tell you." Her hand convulses in mine. "A friend of mine informed me that your cell has been tracked, not only that, whoever has been tracking you was listening to your phone calls."

She gasps. "Martin?"

I nod. "That's what I'm guessing. It's how he knew you'd be at your parents' house."

She gapes at her phone. "Is he still doing it?"

My jaw clenches. "Yes, the man that gave the devices to Martin confirmed that he is indeed still using them and that it was last used less than twenty four hours ago."

"Oh," she whispers, her eyes wide with fear.

"He's not going to get you, Mia. I have a new cell on the way, Aaron's getting it as we speak. I have an address for Martin, once Aaron gets here, he'll be sitting on that place until I'm finished with the Fed."

Her body slumps forward as she releases a ragged breath. "Thank god. Hopefully it means that we can stop him now."

"Yeah, Princess, we're going to stop him. I've not even told you the most fucked up part yet."

"Oh God," she groans.

"Do you remember me telling you about Martin's mom dying?"

She turns to look at me. "Vaguely."

"Well turns out that the woman that we buried wasn't his mom, it was a girl he kidnapped when she was in her teens. She's dead and I'm wondering what else he did to her? But one of my men delved into Martin's background and found out that his parents are still very much alive."

She shakes her head. "Is everything a lie?"

"With him, it seems so. Dad is with them at the moment. He's going to take out some of the rage he has."

She doesn't say anything, her eyes fixated on her cell that's lying on the bed. A look of sheer horror is written all over her face.

"I've moved all your photos to the memory card, so that you won't lose them when you change your cell. Mia, what my dad does, it's what he needs to do." I remind her that this is the business we're in.

"I know, is it bad that I want him to feel what I feel right now? That numbness, that pain, the utter devastation of losing your parents?"

I pull her toward me and she comes willingly. "No, Princess it's not bad, it's natural."

"I don't think it is Hudson, I don't think this darkness that I have is normal. The need for revenge, for his life isn't natural." Her tone hesitant and full of worry.

"Mia, that's what I feel knowing what that bastard did to you, it's my normal. Sometimes we have to embrace the darkness that's fighting to come out. Sometimes we have to let it engulf us. If we don't then we're denying who and what we're meant to be."

She glances at me. "What am I meant to be?"

My hands frame her face. "You're the princess of my organization."

"What does that mean?"

I smile. "It means that once we marry, you'll be queen to my king."

She blinks. "But you've been calling me princess for ages."

My smile widens. "Finally realizing, huh?"

"Do I have to kill people?" she asks quietly and I can't help but laugh. She hits my shoulder. "Don't laugh at me."

"Sorry," I lie, not even in the slightest bit sorry, she's so fucking cute. "No, you don't have to kill people but Mia, once the baby's born, I am going to insist that you take self-defence lessons, along with learning how to fire a gun."

"I want to learn, God, I want our children to learn. I don't want anyone to be in the same helpless position that I was in."

"Children?" I question, remembering her saying only a few hours ago that we'll wait until this baby's born before we decide on anymore.

Her lips twitch. "Slip of the tongue."

A knock on the door, ends the conversation. "Time to go," I tell her as I stand. My cell rings and I look at the screen, it's Aaron. "Yeah?"

"I'm outside," he grunts and hangs up.

Mia follows me to the front door, she grabs the keys of the counter as we pass by it. "We're going to Church," I tell Aaron as I open the door, the smirk that forms on his lips tells me that he's looking forward to it. It's been a while since we've been there and it's been a long time coming.

We walk toward the car, Aaron walking in step beside me. "Any word on your mom, Boss?" he asks quietly not wanting Mia to overhear.

Shit. "Mom's good, she'll be back to normal in no time." I glance back at Mia, she's pulling the front door closed behind her. "Tina didn't make it."

"Fuck, Boss," he whispers, "How is she?"

"About as good as you can expect. She's hurting. Dad's working on taking down Martin's parents and I have Intel on where that bastard is. I'm sorry Aaron, you're going to have to miss church and sit on him. If you see him, follow him."

His back straightens. "Fuck church, there'll be more times that I can attend church. Not every day we find the biggest rat since Benedict Arnold." So much pride in his voice, he knows that me asking him means that I trust him. Since shit has gone south, Aaron has been one of the men that have risen through the ranks, he's been loyal. I respect that and have shown him that his loyalty is seen and have rewarded it.

"Stop at a fast food joint, Mia needs food," I instruct him as I open the back door of the car, waiting for Mia to get into the car. As soon as she does, I slide in next to her, "Ready for this?"

She shrugs. "As ready as I'll ever be." She leans her head against the car and sinks into the seat, her hand reaching over and grasping mine. "We're in this together."

SIX

Mia

SITTING IN THIS HOTEL LOBBY, I'm struggling to come up with how this place has anything to do with church, that's what Hudson told Aaron, they were going to church. Yet, I'm in some fancy hotel. I've searched the Internet and a night here cost upwards of a thousand dollars. I know that Hudson owns this place, he told me when he left me in the lobby and walked toward the elevator. I'm wondering where he's gone. Why would he bring me here and leave me? It doesn't make sense, I'm missing something.

The elevator dings and I glance at them once again, every time they arrive at the lobby I hope that it's Hudson returning but each and every time it's not. A couple walk out hand in hand, the look of love in their eyes as they stare at one another. I know that's something that Hudson and I won't be able to do, we won't be able to be so carefree, we'll always have bodyguards, always have people watching us, protecting us. I don't ever envision it not being that way, not again, not after what has happened. The same way, I don't see Hudson trusting anyone like he did with Martin and Barney, although Barney never betrayed him, he kept things from Hudson, and when the time came to be honest, he wasn't, he evaded the truth. I know that Hudson had him killed but I don't blame Hudson, I blame Martin. If Martin wasn't so hell bent on vengeance, and framed Barney, he'd still be alive. That man has killed a lot of innocent people and it's time he paid the price.

Once again the elevator dings, my head immediately turns to the sound, relief washes through me when Hudson walks out, a smile on his face. He stands by the elevator doors, looking every bit the powerful man he is. I bite the inside of my cheek when he crooks his finger at me, he's instructing me to come to him. How dare he? I'm not a dog. I rise from the chair and walk toward him. As soon as I get close his hand reaches for me.

"You crooked your finger at me," I tell him as I take his hand.

He smirks. "I did." He presses the button for the elevator.

"It was extremely rude." I inform him as we wait.

"I apologize, what would you like me to do in the future?" I know that he's not taking it seriously, and neither am I, it annoyed me and I've told him as much. I shrug, not sure what he should do, anything is better than that. "I'll walk over to you."

"Is everything okay? You were gone a while." I ask as the doors to the elevator open.

Hudson places his hand on the base of my back, directing me past the doors. As soon as he releases me I walk to the back and turn to face Hudson. The elevator is empty and once the doors close, Hudson speaks. "I had to check on the condition of Johnson, while I want you to see my world, there are some things you do not need to see."

His gaze is intense as he looks at me, those deep brown eyes so full of love and affection.

My tongue swipes my bottom lip, coating it so that it's not dry. "How is he?" I don't know why I'm asking, curiosity getting the better of me, maybe?

"Alive, barely injured. He's ready to be questioned. I'm going to ask you once again to stay in the shadows. Whatever you may see you are not to react." The warning is there. So clear to hear.

"I won't I promise I'll stay outside and I'll be quiet." I promise him, just as I did with Macka. I won't go against Hudson not in front of his men anyway. I know that if I challenged him in front of his men it would be classified as disrespect. If his men did it they'd be punished.

He stalks toward me, his hands going either side of my body onto the walls of the elevator, pinning me where I stand. "Made for me," he murmurs gruffly and I feel it all the way in my stomach, where those butterflies begin to swarm. I bite back a groan as his lips touch the shell of my ear, "Never letting you go," he declares and instantly my thighs slam together as liquid pools in my panties. "Mine," he growls and I shiver.

"Hudson," I moan, he can't do this to me, not here. It's not fair, we're about to face his men.

His lips gently touch mine. "I promised you, no more tonight." Even as he says the words I can see the lust in his eyes, he doesn't want to keep his promise. "Anyway, we're here now."

I frown when I realize that we've gone down to the basement. As soon as the doors open Hudson grabs my hand and pulls me behind him. He leads us past the laundry room and towards a steel door. A hundred questions run through my mind but when I see David waiting for us, each one of them are silenced.

"Boss," David says with a nod of his head and I realize that when the men nod their heads to him, it's their way of doing a courtesy, it's a show of respect.

I give David a small smile, my heart hurts for him, he's just lost his wife and he looks a mess. His normally shaved head is starting to grow out, he's light stubble growing into a full beard. His eyes are bloodshot, and his clothes are unkempt.

"My condolences, Princess," he murmurs.

"Thank you," I reply shocked, he called me Princess, only Hudson has so far. I'm not sure that I like it coming from anyone else's mouth. It sounds foreign.

"David, call Rory and find out what the hell is taking them so long," Hudson instructs him and I keep my head down as the steel door opens, Hudson immediately steps in front of me, shielding me in case anyone's looking.

"On it, Boss."

Once we're in the room, I realize why they call it the church, it's an old small offertory, with pews and an altar. I have so many questions and yet no one to answer them just yet. The room is in darkness, only a little light by the alter shining. I move in the shadows to the darkest corner of the room, my eyes on the figure strapped to a pew in front of the altar. He's in his pants, his shirt off and lying on the ground beside him, his arms and legs both restrained with zip wire, a tie shoved into his mouth, no doubt silencing his screams. There's six men in this room, three of them I know, I have seen, they're Hudson's men, Jagger, Liam, and Alex, the other's I've not seen before. Hudson usually only lets those who show their loyalty to him around me.

"Mr Johnson, it's good to see you." Hudson says sarcastically, the men laugh. "Now, are you ready to talk?"

I watch as Mr Johnson's eyes narrow. He says something but it's hard to make out what, as it comes out as a mumble thanks to the tie that's being used as a gag.

"Fine, have it your way," Hudson says and clicks his fingers. Two of the men leave the room, they're gone for a few minutes before they return with a woman being dragged into the room with them, and David looking menacingly as he walks in behind them. "Do you know who this is?" Hudson taunts and I press closer to the wall as they throw the woman to the ground beside Mr Johnson.

"Clive, what have you done?" The woman sobs as she gets to her knees. Mr Johnson once again mumbles something and the woman tentatively reaches up and pulls down his gag. "Why am I here?"

"They want something," he says through clenched teeth, it's then that I notice that his leg is broken. It's twisted in a way that it shouldn't be.

"What? What is it that they want?" she cries.

"Josie, please, just shush, it's going to be okay," he tells her, it's almost as if he knows something, something we're missing. His cockiness reminds me of Macka and how he was confident that Martin wouldn't be found out.

"Okay? Do you know who that is?" she whimpers. "He's a monster, Josie. It's Hudson Brady. He won't hesitate killing us."

"I am right here and I can hear you," Hudson smirks, he loves that people think he's a monster, if they knew the truth, they'd be shocked. Being the boss is only one side of him, the other side is a side he shows to very few, I get to see it every day.

"Mr Brady..." Josie stutters, "Why am I here?"

Hudson's smirk turns sadistic. "You're here because he is a dirty cop."

She gasps. "No, you're mistaken, he's not. Clive is a good man."

Hudson laughs. "He cheated on you and you call him a good man? You're deluded, he's a liar and because of him, innocent people have died. Because of him, my woman was taken."

She shakes her head. "I know that he cheated, but he wouldn't hurt anyone, he wouldn't let someone die."

"Tell her," Hudson demands, his voice deep and unforgiving.

"I don't know what you want me to say." He's a fucking coward, I can tell he's lying, he just won't admit it.

"That you are working with Martin, that you have helped him escape my clutches." Hudson's losing his patience, his words are clipped. Mr Johnson doesn't have long before someone gets hurt and I have a feeling it won't be Clive that will be feeling the wrath of Hudson.

"If he was helping him escape you, how was it a bad thing? A lot of people deserve to live Mr Brady, you don't need to kill anyone," Josie tells him, she's trying to help her husband. I commend that, I'd do the same for Hudson but she's digging herself a bigger whole.

"Let me enlighten you, Mrs Johnson." The way he says her name makes my skin crawl, the anger is palpable. "Your husband," he spits. "Helped a man kill a nineteen year old girl, he also helped him cover up the death of a seventeen year old, a girl who he had kidnapped three years prior, not only that, since then he has set fire to a house, trapping a woman inside, killing her in the process and only last night he shot two innocent women, injuring one and killing another."

She gasps, getting to her feet. "Clive?" she questions, finally she's starting to realize that her husband isn't as innocent as she's been led to believe.

"Josie," Mr Johnson cries, "Listen to me, he's lying."

"Have you helped this man?" she questions, her voice strong, there's no more tears, she's angry. Anger is good, it'll help her see the truth.

When Mr Johnson doesn't answer her, Jagger helps him out, his hand presses down on his broken leg. It snaps and I cringe, God, he's broken it even more. Mr Johnson cries out.

"You'd better answer her Clive, otherwise, there'll be more snapping," Hudson tells him, he's reigned in his anger.

"Fine," he yells. "Fine." He's breathing hard and shallow. "Yes, I've helped him."

"Did you know what he's been doing?" Josie asks and I stare at her in disbelief, why? Why the hell is she asking such stupid questions? There's no way he didn't know about what Martin was up to.

Again, Clive doesn't answer her, his silence speaks volumes.

"Oh God, what have you become?" Josie questions, utter disgust in her voice. "When did you turn into this monster?"

"I was sick of him getting away with everything. The missing men, the enemies that vanished into thin air, and nothing ever traced back to him. He'd come up clean as a whistle every single time. Even his club is legit."

Hudson scoffs. "So you thought you'd work against me? That you'd bring me down?"

"You need bringing down," Clive yells and Jagger presses down on his leg once again, his scream fills the air. "He does, he's evil, and how do you manage to always get away with it?"

Hudson raises his brow. "I have no idea what you are talking about. I've not done anything criminal until this very moment. But who are you going to tell? Hmm? Your colleagues? Once they find out what you have done, the murders that you are responsible for, do you really think they'll put you on the stand to testify against me? My attorney is too good for that, he'll discredit you with just one sentence. Let me make myself very clear Mr Johnson, because of your actions the woman I love was hurt, hurt beyond your comprehension and for that I'll never forgive you." Hudson raises his gun, its aim pointed at Clive.

"What?" Clive blubbers. "Who?"

"You have someone you love?" The softer tone of Josie makes Hudson glance at her, "What happened to her? Did she die?"

"No, she didn't die," Hudson grinds out.

Josie nods. "She was assaulted." It's not a question.

"I'm sorry, how is she doing?"

"Better than I expect, but there's times that she's not. Now because of your husband, her mother was killed this morning." He releases a harsh breath and turns his attention back to Clive. "How many times does she have to take the hit because you're a pussy?"

"I never intended anyone to get hurt, that wasn't my plan."

"What exactly was your plan?" Jagger asks, he's getting angry now. Nothing Clive is saying makes sense, he isn't being truthful, or if he is, he isn't letting us know the full story. It's frustrating as much as it is annoying. This would be over a hell of a lot sooner if he would just say whatever it is he's done or has planned, instead of making everyone even more angry and pushing Hudson to his limit.

"I planned on pushing you to do something illegal, that I'd catch you in the act as you did it."

"So what changed? You haven't caught me as of yet so

what was it that changed?" Hudson grounds out, his gun still aimed at Clive.

"Martin." He breathes. "He kidnapped two women, he hit one of them on the head and she crumpled to the floor, I thought she was dead." He shakes his head. "Things had changed, I couldn't do it anymore."

A gunshot sounds, followed by a thump.

Hudson shoots and I cover my mouth so the scream that's lodged in my throat doesn't escape. He shot Josie, I can't help but stare at her lifeless body, she's slumped on the ground with a bullet between her eyes. Tears sting but I don't let them fall. Why did he kill her?

"Josie!" Clive wails, "You're a coward." He yells at Hudson, "You can go to hell, I'm not telling you anything else."

Hudson stalks toward him. "You were there." His voice deadly, it makes the hairs on the back of my neck stand up. "You were with him when he took the two girls?"

I remember his words, he knew I was hit over the head. He was there? Oh my God, he's meant to protect people, he's meant to be the one that people trust when they're in danger. Instead he was a participant in mine and Lacey's kidnapping. This world is so messed up, he's meant to keep me safe and the man that is viewed as a monster, the one I'm meant to keep away from at all costs is the one that has proven that he'll protect me. Is it any wonder why I'm so at ease with the Boss?

"I asked you a fucking question. Now answer it!" Hudson yells, digging the gun into Clive's chest, causing him to hiss as the heat from the gun burns his flesh. The smell is putrid but I breathe through it.

"Yes, I was there." He spits out.

"You're the reason that they were hurt, that she was raped and the other died." Hudson tells him in a quiet voice. My skin breaks out in goosebumps and I bite back a whimper. That voice is the scariest thing I've ever heard. It's something I never want to hear again.

"No."

"Yes. You should have stopped him," Hudson yells taking a step back. "What did this get you huh? Working for my enemy? Did it make you feel good? Hm? Or did you get paid handsomely for it?"

"Neither," he responds instantly, his voice shaking.

"Then why?" Hudson's out for answers and he's not letting him go without them.

What happened to me affected him more than it did me. Yes, I wake with nightmares, I'm scared that Martin's going to get me again, I can't sleep without the bathroom light on. But I know that once Martin is out of my life that I'll be okay, I'll know that he won't be able to hurt me again. Whereas Hudson, he blames himself. He heard what happened to me and it's chipped away a piece of him. He thinks he's failed me, he fails to realize that he saved me, that because of him I was able to survive what that animal did to me. I don't think we'll ever be able to get that piece back.

"What did you get out of this?" Again his anger is receding, it's weird to watch how close to the edge he comes but he's able to pull himself back.

"He was blackmailing me."

I roll my eyes, isn't that always the motive? God, have some damn backbone. I wonder if it was worth it? Was all of this worth whatever the hell he wanted to keep a secret.

"About what?" Jagger questions.

I glance around the room, each of the men are standing in the light. I'm the only one hidden in the shadows. All of them have their hands on their guns, ready for whatever is coming next, they all have the same look of disgust on their faces.

Clive looks at Josie's body on the floor beside him, "he was blackmailing me about the child I have. The one that was the result of the affair I had. I didn't want Josie to know."

"You have a child?" Hudson laughs, "Imagine what they're going to think about their father?"

Clive struggles against his restraints. "I pray you never have children, to inflict the evil that you are on them."

"My children will know what I am, I'll never pretend to be anything else. Unlike you, a man that acts as though he's one of the good guys when in fact you're no better than I am. Now, what is Martin's endgame?"

A smirk forms on Clive's lips, "To end everyone you care about. He's going to kill everyone you love and then he's going to kill you." He's revelling in dishing out that information.

"That's never going to happen." Hudson tells him and once again lifts the gun. When he pulls the trigger this time, I don't even flinch.

SEVEN

Hudson
———————

JAGGER DRIVES US TOWARD HOME, David's in the front and Mia's head is against my shoulder as she sleeps. The rest of the men are in two other cars, one in front and one behind. Now we know what Martin's end game is, we're going to ensure that nothing happens. The car behind will be turning off soon and heading to the hospital. They're on protection duty for my mom, there's no way that fucker is going to get another shot at her.

"David, did you talk to Rory?" I ask quietly not wanting to wake Mia.

"Yes boss, he said your father was talking to them, that he's been demanding answers and if they haven't been forthcoming he's been forcing those answers out of them."

"Good, has Aaron checked in?" I ask, wondering how long my dad's going to take, the longer he's there the more chance he'll be caught.

"Yes boss, he called just as we were leaving the church. He said to tell you that you were right. He has a visual." David replies and I smile. "Boss, may I ask, what he has a visual on?"

"Martin," I respond and watch as both Jagger and David immediately still.

"We have him in our sights?" David asks cautiously, I know he's dying to get his hands on him.

"Yes, once my father has done his job, we'll be leaving the bodies where he stays. Show him that we can get to his family as well," I reply, wondering if I should have David go to Aaron or not? If I do, can I trust him to reign in his anger and stay hidden? Or will he lose the plot and maybe have Martin run, making us lose him again? "David, once it's done, you'll be with Aaron, watching to see where that fucker goes."

"Boss, when Portia died I vowed I'd extract revenge, I promised her parents that I'd make the man that killed her pay. I'm not going to go against you to get that revenge because I know that once we have him, my promise will be made. I may not be the man to end him, but I'll be part of the reason he's dead," He's reassuring me that I'm making the right decision.

"I respect that, I really do, but I expect you to take the shot if that fucker runs. I'd rather him dead than have him regroup and take more shots at our families."

He nods. "Understood boss, if he does a runner, I'll take him out. If not, we'll bring him in and we can play." His tone is sadistic and I smile, my boys love their blood. Not only that, they love exacting revenge and I'm not one to let them down, except when it's to do with my family.

"Jagger, once my dad's finished, I'll ask him to watch Mia. You'll organize a meeting. Every man is to be in attendance other than Aaron and David. Anyone not in attendance will be put on notice. Once the meeting is done, I want you to have the men sweep the club for bugs. No more shit, we're getting our house in order."

"Will do boss, I'll call Coby and see if he's got anything

we can use in his office. What about your mom, when will she be going home?"

Mia lets out a low moan and I glance down at her, she looks uncomfortable but I'm not moving her. She's strapped in her seatbelt and I'm not risking taking her out of it. "Probably another couple of days. While Martin is out there, she'll have twenty-four seven security."

"Have you thought about moving her into your house until this is over?" Jagger asks, "It'll mean Mia has some company that isn't male, and she'll be looked after if you have to leave."

I have thought about it, but I haven't approached Mia about it yet. "I'll talk to Mia and see what she thinks." While it will be a sensible idea, I want Mia to be comfortable in her own house.

The car behind us turns, we're almost at home. Once I get inside, I'll be fucking happier, although Aaron hasn't said Martin's on the move, it doesn't mean he doesn't have someone watching us. Anything can happen and all of us are on alert.

Jagger pulls into the driveway and I gently wake Mia. "Let's get you to bed." I tell her, as I open the door.

"Hudson," she moans. "You've had it twice already, let me sleep."

Jagger laughs and David's ears turn red, no doubt he's hiding the laughter.

"Mia, we're home," I tell her a bit louder and her eyes open and she gapes at me. Jagger's still laughing. "Come on, let's get you inside."

"I'm sorry," she says sheepishly as I get out of the car.

I hold my hand out for her, she takes it. "Don't worry about it, Princess."

She rests her head against my chest as we walk toward

the door, Jagger's still laughing his ass off and I turn and glare at him.

I turn on the light, Mia buries her head even further into my chest, shielding her eyes from the brightness. "Go to bed baby, you need the rest." I tell her softly, kissing the top of her head.

"Okay," she says through her yawn. "Don't stay up too late." She pulls away from my chest and places a kiss on my lips. "Goodnight Jagger, goodnight David," she says as she walks toward the bedroom.

"Goodnight, Mia," Jagger says, the fucker still has a smile on his face.

Goodnight, Princess," David responds.

She disappears into the bedroom. I walk into the kitchen, opening the fridge, I reach for the beer.

"Hudson." Her shrill scream rents through the air.

Jagger, David, and I are running into our bedroom. My hand on my gun, I come to a stop when I see her staring at the bed. I glance around the room and see it's empty except for us.

"Hudson, he's been here," She whispers.

"Mia, what's going on?" Jagger asks as I try and regain my breath. Christ I thought someone was here.

She picks something off the bed and turns to face me. She hands me the small box and a note. Her entire body shaking, tears fall down her face. God, what the fuck happened? How did this get in here?

I read the note.

MIA,

WE'RE EXPECTING. HOW AMAZING. I NEVER THOUGHT

about being a father before but I'm really looking forward to the idea.

When will we know about the gender? I'd like to know so I can attend the scan.

Please ensure that Hudson is not in attendance. I do not want that man near my child.

I'll be close by, keeping an eye on you.

Here's a little gift for our baby.

ALL MY LOVE,
M.

YOU HAVE TO BE FUCKING SHITTING ME.

Before I can say anything, Jag snatches the note out of my hand. His eyes grow wide as he reads the note. "Mia, you're pregnant?" His eyes watery, and I know he's thinking that what that asshole has said in that note is true. He loves Mia and is hurting for her.

"Yes, she is and that fucker better watch his step. Mia is ten weeks pregnant, we found out today, she had a scan. So get that fucking look of your face, it's not his." I'm going to be fielding this goddamn questions for a long time.

"Congrats boss, another male to take over," David says patting me on my shoulder.

"Thank fuck for that," Jagger sighs in relief. "Welcome to the club man." He pulls me into a hug. "So the little dude is due when? March?"

"I'm not sure, I never asked," I say, and look to Mia to help me out. She's standing there with her hands on her hips, tears falling down her face but she's pissed. "Mia?"

"Since when did we know the gender? Hmm? Last time I checked, I was ten weeks pregnant." There's a bite to her tone, I know she didn't want anyone to know just yet, but there was no way around them knowing. Especially with this fucking gift.

"What's in the box?" David asks, anger lacing his words.

I take the lid of the box and I see red. The fucker bought a fucking teddy bear.

"Can we throw it in the trash?" Mia's voice is small, she's upset, absolutely fucking wrecked. "How did he find out?"

I pull her into my arms. "I don't know, but I promise you he's not getting anywhere near you."

"He'll die before he gets a chance," David vows. "Mia," he says and she turns to face him, it's the first time he's called her by her name, he's called her Princess so far. "I'm going to stay on that fucker's trail, I'll know where he is every second of the day. He's not going to hurt you, or your baby."

Mia pulls away from me and walks over to David, her arms going around him and she pulls him into a hug, sobbing against him as she does. I leave her be, knowing that she's grateful to him, I'm not jealous of it, in fact, I'm relieved that they're developing a friendship. David needs some softness in his life right now. I'm not sure if I'd be so easy if it were any of my other men. Jagger's an exception.

My cell rings, taking it out of my pocket I see that it's dad. About fucking time. "Is it done?" Mia and David pull apart, the hardness he had in his eyes has softened.

"Hello to you too," he replies, but I'm not in the mood. "It's done, you little shit."

"Dad, get here, bring Rory and Cormac with you. David will bring them to the dump site."

"Shit, what's happened now?" He's not as wound up, it seems he's released some of that anger.

"I'll explain when you get here." I end the call and take Mia's hand, leading her into the kitchen.

"Hudson, did you leave the fridge open?"

I ignore the question and grab three beers. I pass one to Jagger and one to David, when I turn to Mia, I see she's staring at me. I sigh, "You screamed, what was I supposed to do? Do you want anything?"

She shakes her head. "No, I'm fine thank you." She follows us into the sitting room as I wait for dad and the others to arrive. Mia curls up beside me as soon as I sit on the sofa, head resting on my arm, I move so that she's tucked up against my body. Once again, she snuggles up closer to me, her head turning into my chest.

"Boss, what are we going to do about Martin?" Jagger asks his eyes on Mia.

"Once dad gets here, the bodies of his parents are going to be dumped outside his hideout along with that fucking gift he gave Mia. Letting him know that he has nothing. He'll run, and Aaron and David will be on his tail." I tell him and glance down at Mia, she's fast asleep. She's had a rough day, with no reprieve at all.

"No doubt that fucker will scurry into the sewers like the rat he truly is," Jagger says taking a sip of his beer, "How long are you going to wait before you capture him?"

"I'm unsure, I'd rather end this now. Getting him at his hideout is stupid, he'll have it rigged. I'm not losing anymore men to this fucker." It'll be a death sentence for my men sending them into it.

"So we tail him and run the fucker off the road." David smirks, his hands balling into fists.

"Yes, take that fucker while he's scrambling."

David smirk widens. "It'll be my fucking pleasure."

A car door slams shut, and we all straighten up. We sit in silence as we wait for dad to come into the house. He doesn't take long and as soon as he walks in the door, he starts demanding answers. "What the hell is going on?" His voice booming which makes Mia moan and turn in my arms. I'll be glad once the morning sickness passes. Glancing at him, I see both Rory and Cormac walking in behind him.

"A lot," David replies as he downs the beer. "You two are with me," he instructs the brothers, and they immediately turn and walk out of the door. Even though I haven't announced that David has moved up the ranks, the men respect him and do what he says. "I'll let Hudson and Jagger fill you in. I've got shit to do." He walks out of the house without looking back.

"So, want to tell me what the hell has happened since I've been gone?" Dad demands, his eyes looking down at Mia. "Is she okay?"

I shake my head. "No she's not." I take a sip of beer, the coldness making it slip down my throat easily. "I read the email from Coby, he told me that Martin has been listening to Mia's calls and tracking her cell. He also gave me his last known location and Aaron has been sitting on him. Shit's about to hit the fan as David's on his way with the bodies and dump them at his hideout."

Dad lets out a low whistle, "Damn, Son." He shakes his head. "Paybacks a motherfucking bitch and he's due to feel karma's sting." He glances between Jag and I. "What am I missing?"

I look down and see Mia's still fast asleep. "Mia's pregnant." I announce and hear the sharp intake of breath, I keep my voice low as I continue. "Before you ask, it's mine. She's ten weeks. Martin somehow has found out about her pregnancy and managed to break into my house and leave a present for her. He thinks it's his child and he's fucking delusional." I shake my head as I remember that fucking note he left for her.

"I'm going to be a grandad? Damn son, you sure know how to put a smile on my face. How's Mia taking things?"

"She's bottling everything up." It pisses me off as I'm unable to help her until she lets it out. "She was scared when she found out she was pregnant that it could be that asshole's. I told her even if it was, I'd support her, and I'd love it as mine."

Dad nods. "Of course you would, Son. Mia's yours and in turn her child would be yours. Just as Mia is mine."

He understands me, something that when I look at Jagger, I don't see. He's confused and that's fine, he doesn't need to understand, it's a moot point. "She had a scan at the hospital, they told her she was ten weeks."

"Good, she doesn't need that fucker in her life and if that baby was his, there's no doubt he'd make her life ten times worse than it is now." Dad says, sitting back in his chair.

"No dad, when he finds out that his family is gone and that the baby he thought was his, isn't. He'll go on a rampage."

Dad tsks. "Fuck, that fucker needs to go down and soon. I'm not having him near Mia or my grandchild." That's a warning if I ever heard one.

"I'm on it," I bite out. "Have some damn faith, yeah? What do you think Aaron and David are going to do? Sit on their damn hands?"

His eyes are narrowed, I know that he wants to say something else but he's biting his tongue. I don't want to hear whatever the fuck it is that he thinks he should say.

"Will you stay here with Mia? I've got to call a meeting."

"Like you even have to ask. I'll guard her with my life," he promises me and I nod. "Go, she'll be fine."

Jagger stands and walks out of the room, he's arranging a meeting with the men.

"I don't think she'll sleep in the bedroom, not after that fucker was in there. So stay out here with her." I gingerly get to my feet, moving her slowly so that she's lying on the sofa.

"I'll stay here and I'll stay awake, nothing is going to hurt her." He stands, taking the blanket from behind him and throwing it over Mia.

"Thanks Dad." I tell him as I finish my beer, "I'll be a couple of hours."

"Don't thank me, you're my son and she's my daughter. Go, I've got her." He pats my back and I turn back to Mia, placing a kiss on her head.

Walking out of the house, I see Jagger's already in the car. He's on his cell, so I climb into the passenger's side and wait for him to end his call.

"Meeting's set, the men are spreading the word like wildfire. I've made it clear if they're not in attendance, they're on notice," he says as he puts his cell in his pocket and drives out of my driveway.

"Good, Dad's got Mia covered."

Jagger laughs. "Poor Mia, she's fucked." I glare at him, it just makes him laugh harder. "She's got you, who's a fucking psychopath who will kill anyone who even upsets her. Me, David, and your father who will gut anyone who hurts her. She has no chance of having peace."

I shrug. "At least she'll be safe." That's all that fucking matters.

EIGHT

Hudson

THE SMELL of smoke hits me as soon as I exit the car. "Fucking hell, a bit morbid, Jag." I comment as I take in the charred remains of the house.

"It was the only place I could think of and David agreed that it would be the best place. They feel the loss, we all do," he tells me, seemingly unfazed that the house was only burned down mere weeks ago. That a woman lost her life as it blazed, our man lost the love of his life in the process.

"Sick fuckers," I murmur as I walk into what's left of the house. The walls are crumbled, there's so much rubble on the ground that it's hard to walk on, I manage to find a way into the building and find my men standing around waiting for me. What used to be the staircase, in pieces beneath our feet.

"I won't keep you long, I have a few announcements to make and then we can get the hell out of here." I glare at Jagger, the smell of smoke is awful, no doubt I'll have to throw my suit in the trash, getting that smell out is almost impossible.

The men chuckle. "Boss," I hear one of them say and watch as Dylan takes a step forward. The man is in his mid-thirties, he's been with us for a while but he's not shown any promise to be anything other than a soldier.

"Yes, Dylan?"

He stops and stares at me. "I know you said that this is a required meeting, anyone who wasn't here was being put on notice."

I sigh, what the fuck is he getting at? I hate this bullshit. "Get to it."

"Boss, Wally isn't here," he tells me and I can hear the wariness in his voice. A hushed murmur falls among my men.

"When was the last time anyone spoke to him?" This isn't like Wally, the man lives for the organization, for my men, for me.

Silence descends as they try and remember the last time they spoke to him.

"Has anyone spoken to him since this morning?" So much fucking shit has happened since then. Again, no one answers. "Right, we'll deal with that afterward." I'll be taking a trip to his house after this meeting. "Now, there have been some developments since this morning."

My men straighten, their heads held high as they stare at me. I'm not sure if the rumors have hit yet, if they haven't I'd be surprised.

"My mom is fine, she made it out of surgery and is on the mend. Tina, however, wasn't that lucky. She didn't make it out of surgery. That's another death on Martin's head."

Curses go around, before each of them bow their heads in a sign of respect.

"Martin's parents are dead, he lied and as a result, they paid that price." They grin, finally, we finally have a small victory. "I've also found out where his hideout is. Aaron and David are sitting on it. His parent's bodies are going to be dumped there, showing him that we know where he is and we will hurt him just as he has us. I've instructed them not to take him there. I'm not risking my men's lives, God knows what he's got rigged, and they're going to take him on the road. He's not going to escape. No more. It's coming to the end."

The men smile, glad that it's coming to a close, we've all been on the back foot with this shit, but changes are going to be made. "Boss, is he coming in alive?" Ronald asks and I smirk, these new recruits are blood thirsty.

"Unless Aaron and David need to use excessive force, he will indeed be coming in alive." I want my go at him, I want to see the life leave his eyes, watch as he finally realizes that I've won. "Now, there's something I need to tell you, and what I say doesn't leave this house."

Their eyes widen, each one of them panicked, wondering what it is that I am about to say.

"Mia is pregnant. Martin believes it's his."

"Fucking asshole. I say fucking take the bastard out," Dylan growls.

"I'd set the fucker on fire," Roland replies.

"Fuck that, I'd attach him to my bumper and drive at full speed," Clayton tells us.

Each one of them come up with a more graphic way of killing him.

"Boss, not that it matters, but is it his?" Kenneth asks, he's the only one that doesn't have a smile on his face. He's been with us for about six months, in the beginning I thought he was a cop, I never have him do anything other than be a part of meetings and work security at the club.

"It's mine." The men all release a ragged breath, one I didn't know they were holding. All except Kenneth, I stare at the man, wondering what the fuck he's playing at. "Not that it matters, though, right?"

His eyes narrow slightly, "Are the rumors true?"

I glance at Jagger, there's something off with this fucker, I knew it from the get go. "What rumors?" There's absolutely no mistaking my tone that he better tread carefully.

He doesn't heed my warning. "That Martin raped Mia."

Every man steps backward as my hand reaches for my gun. He's pushed his damn luck, the man is done. "Who told you that?" There are only a few men in my organization that know what happened and I know that they wouldn't say a word, if they have, they'll pay the price.

He doesn't back down, he's a brave man, there's no doubt about that. "I overheard it."

"Dude," Roland growls, taking a step forward. "You had better wise up." He informs him, and I let him do the talking, right now I'm close to taking my gun and putting a bullet in his head.

"I asked a question," Kenneth replies, a smug smile on his face.

"A question that you had no right asking, now that you have, you best answer the boss' question. Who told you about it?" Roland steps up so that he's face to face. "Answer the damn question, who told you?"

Kenneth's bravado seems to drop, "I overheard it."

"Leave him," I demand, as Kenneth hands reach for his neck. "Kenneth, do you value your life?" I ask and he shrinks back not answering, "Let me rephrase the question. Do you value the life of your wife and daughter?"

His Adam's apple bobs up and down as he gulps, "Y...yes," he stammers.

"Then you had better start talking or I'll start shooting." I don't give a fuck, I'll take his entire family out, I want to know who's been talking about what happened to Mia. I want to know who's got loose lips and can't be trusted.

His next word has my entire body going solid. "Martin."

"When did that asshole tell you?" Jagger says through clenched teeth.

Do we have a traitor amongst us? How did we manage to overlook this one?

Kenneth smiles. "The night he did it."

"Move," I tell Ronald, and he immediately takes a step aside, my gun lifts, "You can go to hell along with him."

That smile widens. "Don't you want to know why he told me?"

Yes. "No, you don't matter to me."

He laughs. "Oh but how I do. You see Hudson, I matter a lot. You thought I was a cop, you have never trusted me and for that, it was easy for me to turn."

I shake my head. "You're full of shit." Fucking jackass. His eyes flash with anger. I laugh, "Oh, did I hit a nerve."

"I turned against you because you have no respect for your men."

I raise my brow. "My men? I have the utmost respect for. I'd die for them as they would me. I don't have respect for lazy, disrespectful, unethical men. That's why I have no respect for you, since the day you came on board, you have shown every one of my men what not to do. Why do you think that none of my men associate with you?"

The shock on his face tells me that he hadn't realized.

"You were dead weight. It's always been a matter of time before you were chopped off."

His eyes narrow. "Fuck you. I hope Martin rapes her again, and that fucking kid of yours."

A red haze forms, and he's gone. I don't even realize that I've lifted my gun and pulled the trigger.

"Fucking prick," Jagger spits as he walks over to Kenneth's body. "He's dead," he informs me and I don't give a shit. "Who the fuck else is a rat? Hmm?" He questions the men and each of them stand tall as if they have nothing to hide. "If it turns out that one or more of you are traitors, I'm personally going to see it that you'll lose your life."

"It's time to go, I've got shit to do. Try and stay out of trouble," I tell them as I turn and leave, "And clean up the body," I demand as Jagger follows me out of the house, "Jag, we're driving over to Wally's house."

He doesn't seem surprised. "Yes boss. What are you thinking?"

"I'm thinking that Wally doesn't miss a damn meeting, he lives for the Brady organization," I tell him getting into the car.

He climbs into the front seat. "Yes boss, but the man's been married less than a week. If that were you and Mia, you wouldn't be leaving the house. You would be balls deep inside of her." He starts the car, just as my men begin to leave the house.

"Watch your mouth," I say through clenched teeth, I don't give a shit if he's my best friend or not, no one talks about Mia that way. He turns on the engine and reverses out of here. "I've got a feeling there's more to this shit than what meets the eye. Why did he tell Kenneth? It makes no fucking sense."

"Unless, Kenneth was a plant all along? Maybe he is a cop after all? He could be one of Johnson's men? I guess the only way we're going to know for certain is ask the bastard when we get him."

I take my cell out of my pocket and dial David's

number. It rings out, no answer. Fuck, I do the same for Aaron's and it's the same. Shit. Fuck. I call Rory, and it rings.

"Boss?" He sounds sleepy like I've just woken him up.

"Yeah, did you do as David had asked?"

"Yes boss. They were dropped off outside his hideout. David told Cormac and I to leave that he had it from there." Gone is the sleepiness, he's fully alert now.

"How far out are you?" I question, my fucking gut screaming that something has happened to Aaron and David.

"Ten minutes, less if I take my bike." He has a Honda CBR1100XX Super Blackbird.

"Take your bike, they're not answering. Find out what the fuck is going on. Call me as soon as you get to that fucking place." I glance at Jagger, his knuckles white from the grip he has on the steering wheel.

"Shit, I'm on it. I'll call you soon." He ends the call and I know that he'll be there within ten minutes, knowing Rory, he'll be there in about seven.

"He's gone?" Jagger asks.

"I believe so, the men aren't answering. We'll know for sure soon enough." My gut's screaming at me that something else is going to happen.

Jagger pulls up outside Wally's house, its pitch black, not a single light on. "They could be asleep," Jagger says and I scoff, he sighs. "Yeah, it doesn't look good."

I'm out of the car, my feet moving as quick as they can, when I get to the door, I know there's something off. My men know about Martin, they know the threat that he brings, they wouldn't leave the damn door ajar. I nudge the door open with my foot, my gun raised as I enter the house. I don't need to move much further than the doorway when I see him. His lifeless body hanging from the banister. Fuck.

"Motherfucker." I don't need to turn to know its Jagger behind me.

"Search the house, find out where Molly is." His wife wouldn't come to the safe house I had for the families, she and Wally had just got married, and they didn't want to be separated. My cell rings and I lower my gun, reaching into my pocket, I see Rory's name on the screen. "Rory."

"Boss, they're gone, all three of them. Aaron's car is still parked here but there's no sign of them. There's blood everywhere."

My cell beeps, indicating I have another call. "Hold on," I instruct him and I put him on hold as I switch the calls. "Yeah?"

"Boss," David says, his breathing labored. "Fucker got the jump on us. I'm sorry. Fucker knocked us out, shit, boss, he bought us to Synergy and set it ablaze. Aaron was still unconscious and has a lot of burns on his body. He's in the hospital being checked out and the firefighters are working on the club now."

Fuck. "What about you?" I ask him.

"What about me?"

I tsk. "David, are you injured?" My tone brooks no argument.

"Not really, I've got a cut on my head but other than that I'm fine."

"Where has Martin gone?" I underestimated him, fuck, I need to call dad, make sure that fucker doesn't go anywhere near them.

"I don't know." He sounds defeated, I know it wasn't his fault. He shouldn't shoulder the blame.

"We'll get him. I'm standing in Wally's house. Looks

like Martin struck earlier today." I don't believe that it was a suicide. No way in hell.

"Fuck. This fuck just keeps on going. We need to hit him hard again."

"Yeah we fucking do." My eyes on Wally, that bastard made it to look as though it was a suicide. "Go to the hospital, get your head checked out and then stay on Aaron."

He doesn't argue with me, "What about Molly?"

I grit my teeth. "No sign of her yet, Jagger's searching the house."

"Fuck, we're back to square one with this shit."

I glance at the floor, hating that all the leverage I had is now gone. "Yeah, we are. This time though, we've dismantled that fuckers operation, he's on his own. He has no plan, and that makes him dangerous but it also means that he's going to slip up. I'm going to be there when he does."

"A-fucking-men to that."

"Get to the hospital and get checked out. That is an order." I end the call and walk toward Wally, as much as I'd love to take him down, I can't. I need to get the evidence, find out if Martin has done it alone or if he's had help.

"Boss, you're going to want to see this." Jagger yells and I turn away from Wally and walk out of the room. "I'm in the bedroom."

I take the stairs two at a time, as soon as I reach the doorway to the bedroom I understand why he wanted me to see it. My body goes rigid at the sight. Molly's lying on the bed naked, her wrists cut and blood soaks the entire bed. Her legs are spread wide apart, and I have to glance away because I know that she's been assaulted, brutally so. Seeing this, it makes everything that he did to Mia come to my mind, I shut down the thoughts instantly, not letting myself go down that rabbit hole. It'll send me spiralling, make me lose my damn mind. Again.

"Boss, it has to be Martin," Jagger says, he's as disgusted as I am. You don't do this shit to innocent women, and you certainly don't do it to my family.

"It's time to go. Call Lazarous, tell him that I want him working this case. I want to know how many men were here and how they managed to overpower Wally." The man was five-feet-eleven and weighed over three hundred pounds, he wasn't an easy man to overpower, it's what has me thinking that Martin wasn't alone. He's got someone else that's working with him.

I walk out of the house, pissed that I've let someone else die. I've lost too many already, way more than we should have. Jagger follows behind me, his voice low as he talks on his cell. He'll see to it that we'll know as soon as the detectives know, as soon as I find out who else is working with Martin, I'll burn them alive.

NINE

Mia

Two Weeks Later

"HUDSON," I moan, his fingers on my nipples, his lips on my neck. My fingers clutching at the sheets beneath us.

"Sssh," he says, not even looking at me.

"Stop teasing," I beg, he's been torturing me for the last twenty minutes. I've come twice and it's not enough. I was awoken by his mouth on my pussy, it was a great way to wake up but now, it's getting too much.

He needs this and I'm going to give it to him. He's hurting, he told me about Wally and his wife, and how he found them. They were buried yesterday. Martin's escaped and no one has any idea where the hell he is. Aaron's still in the hospital, he's in a bad way, his body has been burned badly. I'm not allowed to visit him unless David, Hudson, Harrison, or Jagger are with me and even then it's only for a little while. They all know that I'm pregnant and none of them are taking the chance in case something happens.

"Sssh," he tells me yet again, as he moves down my

body, his mouth at my breasts. My body arches when his teeth bite down on my nipple.

"Please, I need you," I beg once again, my hand wrapping around his dick and I squeeze, loving the way he throbs in my hand. His fingers go to my pussy and my body convulses as he grazes my clit. It's too much, I can't do it again. "Hudson. Please, I need you in me."

He shifts suddenly, I release his dick and his fingers leave my pussy. Within seconds he's thrusting into me. I scream out in pleasure as his cock fills me. "Yes."

His buries his head in my shoulder and thrusts, grunting with every movement he makes. He's not once looked at me, this isn't how he usually is with me. As good as it feels, there's an emptiness with it. He's not present, his mind is elsewhere and I'm an outlet for his anger. His thrusts get harder, each one painful but yet I want more. His grunts get louder, now they're mixed with my moans, I'm so close and from his erratic movements, I can tell that he is too.

He comes on a long groan, within seconds he pulls out of me and I'm left feeling unsatisfied. Turning over in bed, I reach for my phone to check the time, it's almost midday, shit, I promised Jagger, Harrison, David, and Hudson that I'd cook dinner for them. They've all been busy these past couple of weeks, most of the time they're skipping meals and not getting much sleep. I put my foot down, today, they're all taking a break. With Sarah and Allie back in New York as Sarah has a fashion show, Jagger's by himself with no one to ensure he eats or sleeps. The men grumbled about having dinner but I wouldn't listen, I want to do this, it's the only thing I'm able to do.

Hudson's mom has moved in with us, she's been teaching me how to cook. She'll be joining us for dinner and Harrison's not looking forward to it. The man ignores her most of the time, only speaking to her if she talks to him. It's childish and it needs to end, they're grown adults who have a child, they should be civil without making everyone around them uncomfortable.

We buried Mom last week, I spent the next few days in bed, unable to get up. There's not a day that has gone by that I haven't broken down and sobbed. Hudson was with me those days I was in bed, telling everyone that unless someone died or something was blown up, he didn't give a shit. He was spending time with me while I grieved. I love him more than ever, he was my rock to lean on and I don't think I would have made it out the other side had he not been there for me.

I finally got to see Sarah and Allie in person, it was good to just hold them both. I still haven't told her everything yet and I'm honestly not sure if I will. I'm finally getting over it, I'm still not able to sleep with the light off but my nightmares are few and far between. Sarah sat beside me at mom's funeral and held my hand through it all, it was great having both her and Hudson flanking me, both of them offering me support.

My foot hits the bedroom floor just as the bedroom door closes. A lone tear falls as I realize that Hudson's gone, he's not spoken to me this morning. He fucked me as if I were someone he didn't care about, it's something I never want to happen again. I've never felt so worthless, so dirty as I do right in this moment. Picking up my clothes from the bedroom floor, I walk into the bathroom, throwing the clothes into the laundry basket. I switch on the shower, my reflection catches my eye, there's a slight bump now. It's not much but I can definitely notice it. My hands touch my stomach, God, I can't believe that I'm pregnant, as much as everything is up in the air right now, fear and anger taint us all, but this baby is the shining spark through all the hurt that I've been feeling, that we've all been feeling.

Getting into the shower, I let the water cascade over me. I'm mad, I'm hurt, and I'm angry at Hudson, he treated me as if I were a nobody, as if I didn't matter. He fucked me and walked away without saying a word. I bow my head and let the water hit my shoulder blades, loving the way it pounds where all my tension is.

Hands go around my waist and I freeze, "Princess." His voice gentle and soft.

I ignore him and keep my head buried, the water hot against my skin.

"Mia, talk to me."

I scoff. "Like you did this morning?" I remove his hands off my stomach, not wanting him to touch me right now. I'm too angry.

"Baby," he whispers. "Fuck, I'm sorry." He spins me around so that I'm facing him. His fingers caressing my cheek. "I'm an asshole, I fucked up, I'm sorry."

I nod, unable to say anything right now, I don't want to argue. Today was meant to be a good day, a day where we could all relax, or try to anyway and he's put me in a bad mood.

"Mia, please talk to me." He's not used to this, I've never been this angry with him before. "Talk to me."

I glare at him, his face full of remorse. "You made me feel like I meant nothing. You fucked me and never said a word. I never felt as used as I did then." His lips part, it's a direct hit. "I felt as though I could have been anyone, I was just a hole for your cock to fill." I shake my head and turn back around, letting the water cascade down around me again.

His hands grip my hips. "You will never be just a hole for me," he growls. "Yes, I fucked you, but I fucked you with love as I have done every time since we met. In the two years I have known you Mia, you are the only woman I have ever wanted." His lips touch my neck and my traitorous body alights in response. "You are more than the woman I love. You are my everything. Never, and I mean never think that you are anything less than what you are." He spins me around, his lips are on mine, hot, heavy, and dominant. When his tongue sweeps into my mouth stealing my breath from me I melt into him as I always do.

He tears his mouth away from mine. "I fucking love you, Princess and that's never going to change."

All the anger I had has disappeared. I melt into him. "I love you too."

He places a kiss against my head. "I'm an ass, I'm sorry." I nod against his chest. "Let me wash you." He releases my hips and I once again turn so that the water's raining down on me.

His fingers massage my head as he lathers shampoo into my hair. "What happened?" I ask softly, loud enough to be heard over the water.

"I'm frustrated, Mia, I've not been able to track him. I've lost him and that's on me. I should have sent more men to take him that night that Aaron was burned." He confesses to me. "I'm pissed that because of this fucking feud he's made, that a lot of people have died. People you love have died. You are innocent in all this and yet, you're the one that has been affected by this the most."

"That's not on you, Hudson. None of this is your fault. You didn't have a choice that Martin was bought into your life. You made him feel welcome, you made him a part of your family, your inner circle. You are a good man, Hudson."

He laughs. "Princess, you have a funny mind-set if you believe that I'm a good man."

I shake my head. "You're not the definition of what most people would call good. But in your world, you treat your men with the utmost respect, you treat them like family. You would do anything for them just as they would for you. You are gentle and loving with me but with your enemies, you're vicious and unforgiving. I don't see what's wrong with that."

"You're an enigma," he tells me as he washes my body with my loofah.

"I'm curious about something."

His hands stop on my back. "What's that?"

"You're a drug kingpin, and I've not heard one mention of drugs, why is that?" It's something that's been playing on my mind, does he not tell me about it? Or does he not do it anymore.

His hands continue to rub the loofah over my body. "Princess, I told you there would be stuff about my work that we won't talk about and that's the product side of things. At the moment, it's on the back foot while I find Martin."

That makes sense. "So you're still selling them?" There's no judgement at all, I'm merely curious.

"Yes Mia, I'm still selling them. It's something that I'm good at, it's something that is extremely profitable." There's an edge to his tone.

"I was curious, Hudson that's all. Can Martin get to the product?" He already set Synergy alight. Thankfully, the firefighters were on scene early and managed to contain it. It'll take a couple of weeks at least to get it fixed and opened again.

"No, he can't. When I began to distrust everyone, I had everything moved. Since then I have only told four people where the product is and those are David, dad, Jagger, and Aaron. I trust those four implicitly as you know, they wouldn't be guarding you if I didn't." I love that he's so open and honest with me, it may have taken a while but it's good that he's letting me in.

"I overheard you and Harrison talking last night," I say sheepishly, I turn around and face him, he doesn't falter, he continues to wash my body. "Do you honestly believe that there's someone else helping Martin?"

"Yeah, I do believe there is. I'm unsure of who it is, if it's one of my men, there will be hell to pay." His hands stop, and he smiles. "There you are, you're all clean."

"Thank you," I whisper as I look down at his cock, it's thick and long, nudging my thighs, almost as if it's begging to be let in.

His fingers caress my skin as he moves even closer to me, his breath ragged hot against my body. "Mia?" He questions and I know he's asking me if it's okay.

"Take me." I whisper, my lips touching his. He doesn't need to be told twice, he lifts me, my legs circling his waist as my arms wrap around his neck. His cock slowly slides into my pussy, filling me inch by inch.

"Thank you for a wonderful dinner, Mia," Harrison says, getting to his feet. "I've not had a proper cooked meal in a long time."

I laugh. "Mom never really liked cooking."

He smiles and for the first time since Mom died, it reaches his eyes. "No she didn't. Hence why I've not had one in a while." He's reminiscing about her, it's something I love, we have a bond, she's alive in the both of us and I have someone to talk to about her.

Marline scoffs. "If you'd kept your dick in your pants, you'd have had one every night."

I shake my head as I watch the happiness Harrison had vanish before my eyes. Anything that Harrison says she always says something to belittle him or to start an argument so far Harrison has bitten his tongue and let all the remarks and comments slide. This time she's gone too far, I thought she was moving on from what happened but every time they're in the same room she brings it up. I understand that she's hurt and betrayed but it has to stop.

"Marline," Harrison says with a bite to his tone, he's pissed and I completely understand.

She huffs, crossing her arms over her chest. "If that woman hadn't have gotten her clutches into you, we'd still be together. No one liked that damn woman, not even your son," she spits out in anger.

I push away from the table, my chair scraping against the floor. I reach for Harrison's empty plate.

"Mia," he says softly, I see the worry in his eyes.

I shake my head, I don't want to talk about it, hell I don't want to hear it. She may not have liked my mom, but I loved her and so did Harrison. "She's dead," I say past the lump in my throat, "she's gone and she's never coming back," I tell him and he rises to his feet, just as Hudson pulls me into his arms. I look at Marline, she doesn't look the least bit sorry. "You may not have liked her, Hudson may not have liked her, but Harrison loved her, I'm sorry that hurts you but he did and she loved him. I loved her, she was my mom." I pull away from Hudson and walk into the kitchen, needing to get the hell away from everyone.

"Mia, I'm sorry that I upset you," Marline says and I sigh, so much for getting away from it, she's followed me into the kitchen.

I turn to face her, not an ounce of sincerity on her face. "It's fine." I lie, not wanting to argue, I have to live with her and it's not worth the hassle.

"I understand that she was your mom, but Mia, she hurt a lot of people."

I sigh. "A lot of people? No, she hurt you." Her eyebrows raise in surprise. "You're entitled to be hurt and angry, but there has to be a time when you come to terms with what has happened and move on. Harrison betrayed you, your marriage, he found someone else and moved on. I can't imagine how that felt, but he's apologized, he's sorry for hurting you, you can't punish him for the rest of your life, it's not fair to him or you, and it's not fair on Hudson. You are both his parents, he loves you both. But right now, he's having to choose between you."

She gasps in outrage. "No he isn't. I have never made him choose."

I shake my head. "The constant sniping, the remarks, the comments. He hears them all, you can't be around Harrison so obviously Hudson will choose which one of you he'll be around at certain times of the day. You're staying here, so that means when Hudson wants to talk to Harrison, he'll leave so it doesn't cause you any hurt."

She glares at me. "Well how did that ass end up here for dinner?"

"I invited him, I invited them all for dinner. They have been so busy focused on trying to get Martin, to restore Synergy that most days they'll go all day without eating. Today, I wanted them to have a day where they could relax and have something proper to eat." Obviously that hasn't happened with them listening to her bitch all day.

"Oh."

"It won't happen again. I'm sorry," I tell her and turn back and fill the dishwasher.

"Please don't apologize. I'm the one that should be sorry. I am truly sorry I hurt you, I never intended to. Whenever I'm around Harrison, all that anger I had resurfaces and it's like verbal diarrhea, sometimes I don't even know what I'm saying. I just spew everything in hopes of hurting him, so that he'll feel a tenth of the hurt he caused me."

I turn back to her, she looks so vulnerable. "I get that, I really do. If Hudson did to me what Harrison did to you, I'd be devastated. I'd cut off his balls." She laughs at my words. "I don't think Harrison meant to hurt you, he was being selfish and thinking of himself."

She walks toward me, stopping just in front of me. "I didn't really hate your mom, I was jealous of her more than anything. She was beautiful and confident, you remind me so much of her. As much as I hate to admit it, her and Harrison really did belong together. Whenever I saw them together, their happiness radiated off them."

I smile. "Yeah it really did."

She pulls me into a hug. "Just as you and Hudson do, your happiness is infectious. It's clear to see how much love you both have for one and another. That baby of yours is going to be spoilt."

"I know, if it's a boy, Hudson's men are going to take him under their wing and if it's a girl. God help her, they're going to make sure no one ever goes near her."

Marline laughs. "Yep, that's what they do, it's what they've always done." She releases me and the smile she has falls, "I need to apologize to Harrison." I'm shocked, that's something that I never thought would happen. "I really did go too far, what happened between us, is exactly that, between us and it shouldn't be played out for everyone to see." She kisses my cheek and leaves the kitchen, my heart goes out to her, it mustn't be easy apologizing to the man that broke your heart and tore away everything you had worked hard for.

I continue cleaning up, not wanting to be present when

Marline apologizes. Hands go around my waist and I instinctively lean back. "Whatever you said to her, worked Princess, for the first time in years they're actually getting along."

I smile. "Good, it's time they put the past behind them."

"Love you, Princess," he whispers as he caresses my stomach.

TEN

Hudson

Two weeks later

TODAY'S the day that I finally get to see my baby. Mia's sixteen weeks pregnant and her body has subtly changed. There's a tiny bump, to everyone else it's not noticeable, but to me, who knows her body intimately, I see it, I feel it, I fucking love it. Her breasts have also grown, as has her appetite.

Martin hasn't surfaced yet. The fucker has gone to ground and I am certain someone is helping him, I've yet to find out who and thankfully Coby's back in town and I have a meeting with him this evening. The good thing about Martin being in the wind is that fucker hasn't been able to kill anyone else. Detective Lazarous has informed me that they found two sets of fingerprints in Wally and Molly's house, neither are in the police database. Thankfully having Lazarous on my payroll means that he's sent me an image of those fingerprints so that I can check them against my employees. Jagger should be getting those this morning, he and David have been instructed to see who those prints belong too.

Mom and dad both wanted to come today but I didn't want them to. Call me selfish, I don't give a shit. Not only do I not want to share this experience with them, I also don't want Mia to feel excluded, both of her parents are dead, it would be a bigger reminder that they're not here to share this life changing experience with her. Mom's pissed but Dad understands, he's seen Mia while she was grieving and he agrees that it should be the two of us at the scan. Mom hates being told no, so she's acting like a petulant child, she's moved out of our house and back home. I've got Rory on her making sure that she's okay.

Aaron is home now, he has to keep going back to the hospital for check-ups. He's up and about, he's pushing himself hard so that he'll recover. He's got third degree burns on the back of his body, thankfully, those on his leg aren't as severe as those that are on his back. He's had three surgeries on his back and his arms, the skin grafts seem to have worked and the skin is a pinkish color which the doctors wanted. He'll never be the same, that's for sure but I know Aaron, he'll come out the other side of this stronger than ever before.

Today, I have a secret plan, one that will come into effect this afternoon. Everyone has been notified except Mia, I have no doubts that this is what I want and I'm certainly not going to stop it just because that asshole's on the loose. My men have been told that I don't care what they're doing, they are to be in attendance. It's time to relieve the stress and a celebration is the perfect way to achieve that.

"Hudson, are you ready?" Mia shouts and I smile, we've over an hour until our appointment but she wants to go now, she's more excited than I am and she's already seen the baby. She walks into the kitchen, a pair of denim shorts on, with a white tank top. She looks sexy as fuck, a bright smile on her face. "Earth to Hudson?" She waves her hand in front of my face as she walks up to me. "Are you even listening?"

I grab her hand and pull her toward me. "Yes, I am indeed listening. You look gorgeous."

She rolls her eyes. "Flattery will get you everywhere. Are you ready?"

I kiss her lips, they're soft and sticky, she's put lip gloss on. "Yes, but you need to relax."

She shakes her head. "You weren't listening to me yesterday were you?"

I smirk. "I was." I wasn't.

Her eyes narrow. "Then where are we going?"

"You're getting a scan." Too easy, I may not have been listening, but I do know what we're doing and where we're going.

"And what will we find out?"

I frown, find out? "We're going to see the baby."

She pulls away from me and grabs the keys off the counter. "Yes Hudson, we're going to see our baby, we're also going to find out the gender." She's at the front door, ready to leave.

Wait, what? "We are?"

She nods. "Yes, we are, now move your ass." She demands and laughs as I run toward her. "Put me down," she yells as I sweep her into my arms.

"Nope," I say popping the P. I carry her out to the car, she opens the door and I gently place her into the seat. "Strap in, Princess, we're going to see our baby." Her smile shines brightly, and it's so fucking contagious.

We're over forty minutes early for our appointment, I hate waiting, and this place is filled with kids and pregnant women. I'm the only man here, it pisses me off to see the heavily pregnant women sitting alone. I understand that they may have to work, but fuck, this is your kid, surely you can take a couple of hours off to be here for your wife and kid. The door behind us opens and a woman comes in, her stomach big and low, it's a wonder she can even walk with it. Her husband holding her and walks her to a seat before going to check in, I didn't realize just how big women can get while pregnant. I'm slightly worried that something will go wrong, Mia's slim frame won't be able to hold it.

"Will you do that for me?" Mia whispers, her focus on the couple that just walked in.

I look to see what she's talking about and see that the man's helping the woman up out of her seat. "Obviously." I reply.

She smiles. "Good, would you shave my legs too? It'll come to a point where I won't be able to see my feet."

I smirk. "Sure, I'll shave whatever you need me to."

She hits my shoulder, "You're such a perv. God, Hudson, we're around kids."

Before I have a chance to answer, we're called in. Mia grips my hand tightly as we follow the doctor, she's nervous now, we both are. As much as I tell her that I want a boy, as long as both she and the baby are healthy, that's all that matters.

Mia lies on the bed and I wait, the doctor is talking to her but I'm not really listening. Mia's hand is still gripping mine. "It's going to be okay," I reassure her and she gives me a squeeze.

The doctor places some gel on Mia's stomach and runs a wand thingy over it and the air is filled with a whooshing sound, followed by a whoomping.

"That's the heartbeat," Mia tells me, I look down at

her and see the tears shining in her eyes. I know that they're happy tears.

The doctor looks at the screen, she takes a while just looking over it, so much so that I'm starting to worry. "Is everything okay?"

The doctor smiles. "Yes, I'm just checking on your baby's organs, everything is developing as it should. You're right on track Mia, your due date is March twenty third."

Holy shit, that's so far but yet so fucking close.

"Can you tell the gender?" Mia's voice is soft but hopeful.

The doctor smiles wider. "Of course, would you both like to know?"

"Yes," we say in unison, I didn't think it bothered me about not knowing, but now that I'm here, I'm dying to know.

"Congratulations, you're having a boy." She moves the wand, her finger pointing at the screen, "See there, that's the umbilical cord and that…" She points to the little line on the screen. She laughs. "He's flashing us, he wants us to know that he's definitely a boy."

I kiss Mia's lips, the wetness and saltiness makes me realize that her tears are falling. "Why are you crying?"

"I'm so happy." She kisses me. "Thank you," she whispers.

"Why are you thanking me? I'm not the one carrying our son." God, son, it feels good to say that.

"Because you've given me everything," she whispers, I watch on horrified as she bursts into heart wrenching sobs.

I glance at the doctor, to see her smiling. "It's normal, her hormones are all over the place." She hands me something. "Here's something to show the families."

I look down and see a scan picture. Fuck, I can't wait to show my dad, he'll be made up. "Thank you, Doc." Mia moves her legs so that they're dangling off the bed, she's ready to leave now, her eyes on the scan picture. Thankfully, she's stopped sobbing.

The doctor passes Mia some tissue to clean the gel off her stomach. "You're welcome, take your time, and I'll see you both soon."

"Hungry?" I ask as we get into the car. We've got a few more hours until I can unveil the surprise.

"Yes. Starved." That's her usual response these days, she's loving blueberry pancakes, I'm sick of them, she had them every day. If she's not with me she'll get one of the men to bring her some, she even brings Aaron them when she goes to visit him. He's threatened to move if she keeps bringing them.

"IHOP?"

Her nose turns up, "Ugh, no, I want gumbo."

I frown. "Gumbo? Princess, we're in Cali not New Orleans."

She shrugs. "There's a soul food place not far from where Synergy is. Your dad got some food from there yesterday."

Fucking dad. "He did?"

She nods. "Yes, he told me Aaron didn't want pancakes and we stopped off to get him some food."

She shrugs. "I didn't realize I'd been making everyone hate pancakes."

I look at her, wanting to see her reaction when I say this. I don't want her to feel like she can't have anything just because the guys are sick of it. "Princess, you want pancakes? We'll get pancakes. I'll eat them every day, five times a day if you want them."

She smiles at me. "No, it's okay, ever since Harrison got the food for Aaron, I've been wanting it." Her cheeks flame. "It smelled so good."

"Wait, you haven't tried it yet?" She shakes her head, a cute little smile on her face. "Okay, let's go get you some Gumbo."

I put the car into drive and head towards the restaurant that sells gumbo funny I've never had any either so it'll be a new thing for the two of us

My cell rings just as Mia and I enter the restaurant. "Go ahead and order, get two of whatever it is you're getting. I'll be there in a minute," I tell her reaching into my pocket and taking out my wallet. I give her a fifty, she takes it and walks into the shop, her ass swaying as she does. Putting my wallet back into my pocket I pull out my phone and see that it's Jagger that's calling. "Yeah?" I answer it, my eyes on the inside of the restaurant, I keep an eye on Mia as she's ordering.

"Everything is setup, boss. The caterers are ready, Sarah has gone all out on decorating the reception room, not to mention the church, she also has Mia's dress waiting." I can hear the smile in his voice.

"Good, what about that other thing we spoke about?" I glance at my watch, two hours remaining until everything falls into place.

"Yes, that's done, it looks fucking amazing. Although I should punch you, it made Sarah cry."

I smile, if Sarah cried, Mia's going to cry. "Mia's just getting some food."

He makes a gagging sound. "God, she needs to lay off those pancakes."

I smirk. "She's getting gumbo."

"Thank fuck. I thought she'd give birth to a damn pancake the way she was inhaling them."

"Jagger," I warn. He's right though, she was consuming a hell of a lot of them, I'm just grateful that she's getting something different.

"Right. I've got shit to do, see you later." He ends the call just as Mia exits the restaurant.

"Everything okay?" she asks softly. Every time my phone rings she tenses, she's waiting for Martin to hit, for us to find out what he's done next. We all are, it's fucking weird that the asshole has gone silent. It's not sitting right. Tonight, Coby and I are having a meeting, we're going to find that fucker and end him.

"Yeah, Princess, everything's fine. Just Jagger, I had him in a job and that was him checking in."

Relief washes through her, happiness shines so brightly in her eyes. "Did you tell him that we're having a boy?"

I shake my head. "No, Princess, I didn't. I thought we'd do it together." I wink as I take her hand. We walk back to the car and I help her in, "I've a surprise planned. Once you've finished eating, I'll show you it."

She smiles. "What sort of surprise?" I close the door on her and walk around to the drivers side. "Hudson, what is the surprise?" she asks, but I don't answer her as I slide into the car. "Hudson?"

I start the car and put it into drive. "Mia, it's a surprise. That means that you don't get to find out until I'm ready. So just wait, okay?"

She glares at me but nods. "Okay, I'll wait. Do you think we'll be able to go to visit mom and dad tomorrow?" she asks softly, she's not been to the cemetery since Tina was buried.

Thankfully there's not a lot of traffic, we'll be home in no time. "Yeah, Princess, we'll go and see your mom and dad."

She takes my hand, giving it a squeeze. "My dad would have loved you."

I laugh. "I doubt that very much."

Her giggle is like a little bell, I love that fucking sound.

"He may not have liked what you do for a living, but he would definitely love you for the way that you love me. The way you treat me. It's all any father could ever want, if we had a daughter, wouldn't you want someone to love her the way that you love me?"

"Yes princess I would, although she won't be dating until she's at least thirty."

She splutters. "Thirty? Hudson, that's unreasonable."

I shrug. "I don't give a shit if that's unreasonable. I know what men think, and there's no way my daughter is going to be doing anything until she's married."

Mia laughs. "Oh God, you're insane!" She cries. "What about Hudson Junior? Will he have to wait until he's thirty?"

"Don't be ridiculous, why would he? He can date whenever he wants."

"You're crazy. Like certifiable. Hudson, that's sexist!" She tells me like I have no idea, "I found the love of my life at eighteen. I wouldn't change that for the world."

"Yes, and if you hadn't have managed to somehow sneak into my club then we wouldn't have gotten together and that would have been a fucking travesty. Having said that, you shouldn't have been in my club, you damn well shouldn't have gone home with someone you didn't know."

She gasps. "I went home with you. We're not having a girl so the point is moot. I'm not arguing with you." She turns to look out the window and I know that I've put my foot in it. I've upset her.

"Mia…"

She shakes her head. "Leave it. It's okay." Her voice is small and I'm pretty sure I hear tears in her voice. I've definitely fucked up.

ELEVEN

Mia

I'M IN ABSOLUTE SHOCK, I can't believe this is happening. "How?" I ask Sarah as she pulls me into a room off the side of the church entrance.

"He's had it planned for a few weeks, everyone has been under strict instructions not to say anything. I swear he'd have killed anyone who would have spilled the beans." Her smile is so wide, I can't help but follow suit. "Mia, he has gone all out. He's not spared a cent in making this everything you could have ever wanted." She reaches for the dress bag that's hanging up and begins to unzip it.

When I see it I gasp. "Oh my God, Sarah how did he know?" I can't believe he actually bought me the dress I had wanted since I was a little girl. From the way it's strapless, to the diamantes, all the way to the fishtail skirt, everything about it is exactly as I had dreamed.

Sarah laughs, "Mia, we've talked about our dream days since we were thirteen years old. There's nothing about this day that I don't know."

My eyes widen. "You? You did all this?"

She shrugs. "You're my best friend Mia, I'd do

anything to make sure that your big day is everything you've ever wanted." Tears shine in her eyes, "Mia, you've been my rock, every single time I felt like giving in, all I had to do is call you. You'd remind me of everything I was fighting for, working towards. You are my sister and I love you with all my heart, I just wish you felt the same."

My tears fall, I've been such a bitch, I've held so much back from her. "Sarah…" I croak.

"Mia, I know something happened to you, I can see it in your eyes."

I wipe the tears. "I didn't want you to think differently of me."

She takes my hands, "Mia, that's never going to happen. You are my guardian angel. Nothing you could tell me would ever, ever, make me think of you differently."

"While I was in that basement…" I look to the floor, shame running through me. "Martin raped me." I shudder at the words. "He shot Lacey, I was tied up, I couldn't save her. By the time I got free, it was too late." Pain bursts into my chest as I remember that day, the tears once again fall and I don't think there will ever be a time that I don't think about what happened to her and not shed a tear.

Arms go around me, squeezing me tightly. "I thought it was something like that. Mia, if I ever get my hands on that bastard I'm going to kill him. He's hurt you and I hate that, but Mia, no one and I mean no one will ever think of you differently. You are amazing, strong, and beautiful, what he did to you, wasn't a reflection on you but him. He's an animal and the day he dies will be the day that we all smile."

"I love you," I whisper pulling her closer to me, I should have known that she wouldn't have thought I was weak or stupid. Just as if this had happened to her, I wouldn't have thought any differently about her.

"I love you too, but Mia we need to get you ready. You've got a wedding to get to."

I smile, I can't believe this is happening. "Okay, but I really do love you."

She rolls her eyes at me. "I love you too doofus. Now get dressed." She reaches for the dress. "We can't leave Hudson waiting too long. He'll be bursting through these doors soon enough." Laughter bubbles up and I can't help but laugh, I can just imagine him getting annoyed and coming to find me.

Sarah helps me into the dress, it feels amazing and fits perfectly. My mouth forms into an O shape when I look at myself in the mirror, I've never looked so beautiful. The dress fits like a glove, it accentuates each of my curves as well as showing off my bump. I sit while Sarah does my hair and makeup, each moment passes the more the anticipation builds, I'm about to marry the man I love more than anything in this world. My hair is down and curled, it's something I've not done to my hair in a while, Sarah's taken the hair that usually frames my face and pinned it to the back of my head with a diamante studded hair pin, it matches my dress. The makeup is minimal, which is good because I have a feeling that I'll be crying throughout the ceremony.

"Ready?" Sarah asks once she's finished getting me dolled up.

"So ready." I breathe.

"You look beautiful Mia, your parents are going to be so proud of you." She tells me, her eyes watery. "I know they're looking down on you today, just as Lacey is."

I nod. "I know, I wish they were here."

She points to my chest, "They're in there Mia. They are always with you. Let's get you married."

Walking out of the room, I'm pleasantly surprised to

see Harrison. He has a smile on his face, and wearing a sharp looking suit. "You look handsome." I tell him with a smile.

"Mia you look gorgeous." He whispers pulling me into his arms. "Mia, I know that you'd wish to have both of your parents here today. If I could, I'd bring them back in a heartbeat."

My heart melts, I know where Hudson gets his sweet side from. "I know, but having you here is like having a piece of mom with me."

He gives me the saddest smile I've ever seen. "Mia, you can say no, but I was wondering if you'd like me to walk you down the aisle?"

The tears that haven't long dried up, unleash again. "I'd love that, thank you so much."

He holds out his arm for me to take. "I'm honored Mia. You have made my son happier than I have ever seen him. I know that your mom loved you very much, you were her pride and joy. As much as she griped about Hudson and his job, she loved you two together."

I take his arm. "I'm not sure about that."

He pats my hand. "Mia, I was with your mom the night before she died. I went to check on her, as much as your mom and I argued we loved each other very much. That night we finally had a heart to heart, everything that was on our minds we aired."

I swallow past the lump in my throat. "You two were getting back together."

He nods. "Yes, we were. Your mom admitted that she was jealous, she missed so much time with you. When you came home this summer, it was supposed to be a way for the two of you to get closer. But you found Hudson again and your mom didn't know how to handle it. Everything she had planned vanished. She watched her baby girl grow into a beautiful young woman right before her eyes and she couldn't deal."

It hurts knowing that he and mom had gotten things patched up, that they were happy and ready to work through everything. Knowing that she was happy for Hudson and I means the world. "Was she happy?" I ask through the limp in my throat.

"Yes, she really was. She told me that she was going to apologize to you and Hudson, find a way to make it up to you both. Mia, your mother made mistakes but never ever doubt that she loved you more than anything." He kisses my cheek. "Now let's get you in there before my son sends out the search party."

I face forward as Sarah walks ahead through the double doors and into the church. The wedding march rings out and I smile. An instant calm washes over me and Harrison and I take a step into the church. My gaze immediately goes to Hudson. He's staring at me, his entire body tight as I walk toward him, not once tearing his eyes off me. His drinking me in and I love the carnal look in his eyes, a look that he has only for me.

Harrison kisses my cheek as I take Hudson's hands. "We're already family Mia, you're my daughter. I'll do everything in my power to protect you."

"Okay old man, can I marry her now?" Hudson grunts, he's still tense.

"Relax, she's here," Harrison says in a low voice so that only Hudson and I can hear him.

I squeeze Hudson's hands, wanting him to look at me. Immediately his gaze returns to me. 'I love you.' I mouth to him and his body relaxes. Harrison walks away, leaving me and Hudson standing here.

When the priest begins to talk, I listen intently all the while keeping my gaze on the man that's about to become my husband. The way his dark brown eyes look so light, so happy, so full of love. The priest talks about the holy sacrament of marriage and what it means, I let his words wash over me. I want a marriage where we're both equals, where our love can conquer anything. I don't want to be the woman, I want to be his woman. I want the world to know that while Hudson rules the criminal underworld, I'll rule by his side. I will stick by him with everything he is, he is my all and I'll protect that and protect us. In just five short months, we'll go from newlyweds to newlywed parents. It's going to be such a drastic change but one that I'm looking forward to, I can't wait until we hold our little boy in our arms.

When it comes to the vows, I'm shocked that Hudson has written his own. As soon as he begins my heart fills with so much love and hope.

"I'll love you till the day I die.
I'll protect you with my very last breath.
I'll cherish you until the end of time.
You are everything I could have ever wanted
With you I am stronger than ever
Forever you'll be my queen."

Tears fall at his words, he's so sweet. I reach out and take his hand, squeezing it letting him know just how much he means to me, how much his words meant.

"I didn't know, I don't have any vows written." I whisper, feeling inadequate, he's spent so much time writing those vows and here I stand before him with no words.

"That's okay, Princess," he replies, bringing my hand to his mouth. "You can do the regular vows." He tells me.

I shake my head. "No, I'll just wing it." he laughs but I ignore it and begin to say what I feel.

"You're my biggest protector.
My biggest supporter
With you I feel loved, cherished, and wanted.
With you, I have no fear, no anger, no pain.
You are without a doubt the best man I have ever met.
You are my world, my love, my happiness.
You are my King."

His eyes widen at my words, they're bright and shining with unshed tears. My big bad man is showing his soft side for the world to see. His hand tangles in my hair and he pulls me toward him, his mouth descends on mine. As soon as his tongue sweeps into my mouth, I whimper. This kiss is hot and heavy.

The priest coughs and Hudson pulls away, his brown eyes dark and full of lust, his smile is wicked and salacious. My gaze is focused on him, I'm enthralled by him, like he's hypnotized me. Once I hear the words, "You may now kiss the bride," my entire body melts, I am his, just as he is mine. Hudson's lips once again descend on mine. The cheers and hollers that go around the church are muted by our kiss.

"Mine," Hudson growls against my lips. "All mine."

"Just as you are all mine." I breathe. "I can't believe you did all of this."

He smiles. "I couldn't hold off any longer, I had to make sure you were mine Mia, forever."

He takes my hand and we turn to face the crowd, everyone who we love is standing with us. Jagger, Sarah,

Allie, Harrison, and Marline sitting in the front row. David and Aaron on the other side and all of Hudson's men behind them. Every pew is taken up with a smiling face, each one of them happy for both Hudson and I. We walk out of the church, hand in hand, my heart is filled with so much love. I've never been as happy as I am in this moment.

"Mia, Hudson has one last surprise for you," Jagger tells me.

Glancing around the reception, all the men have their heads bowed. They know what's about to happen, they know what's to come and I'm scared.

"Mia…" Just one word takes my breath away, looking to Hudson, I see that his eyes are on me. He reaches for my hand and I intertwine my fingers through his, squeezing hard as more words come. "I'm so proud of you baby girl."

The tears fall. "How?" I gasp, unable to quite comprehend how he has my father's voice playing right now. Something I have always wanted to hear again but never thought would be possible.

"Your mom had videos of you and your father. We managed to take the audio and make this," Hudson whispers, "Keep listening princess, there's more."

"I love you baby girl, you're always with me." Warmth runs through me at listening to the words he always used to say to me.

Mom's laughter fills the air and I look to Harrison, his hand goes to his chest and he rubs, almost as if he's trying to ease the pain. "Always with us. Both of us," she tells me and I shake my head, that's what she would say whenever my father would say that he loves me and that he'll always be with me. It was something they would laugh about.

"Mia, you have turned into a beautiful young woman. I am so proud of who you have become." I frown, I don't remember my mom saying this, when did she? "You and Hudson are perfect together. I know that you two are going to be extremely happy together."

My tears fall and I let them, why have I not heard that before? Where did it come from?

"Always remember that we are with you. We love you." Both mom and dad say in unison.

I hear sniffing and turn to see Sarah crying too. I didn't think that Hudson could get any sweeter than he was, but this, this is more than I could have ever imagined.

"Princess," he says and I try my hardest to pull it together, the tears are falling thick and fast, I'm trying to make my breathing even but it's no use, I'm sobbing and there doesn't seem to be any let up. "Fuck."

"Told you, they'd cry," Jagger says, as Hudson pulls me into his arms,

"By the way, where's the food?" Jagger shouts.

"Jagger!" Sarah yells, "Don't be so selfish."

I laugh, those two are so loud but yet so beautiful together. I'm glad they've gotten back on track.

"That's what I like to hear, I didn't intend to make you cry," Hudson whispers in my ear.

"They were happy tears. I've always wanted to hear my father's voice one last time and you gave that to me. It was the best present I could ever have. Not only that, you gave me my mom's laughter, you gave me her happiness."

"You have to thank my father. He and your mom had a conversation, and she recorded a message for you afterward, dad said she was practicing what to say to you. I think that having her last words to you was fitting." He kisses my head, "I have it saved onto a flash drive, if you want it, we can transfer it to your phone."

"I want," I whisper, more than anything.

"First thing tomorrow morning I'll do it. Tonight, I have more important things to do." His hands slide across my stomach, his dick hard against my ass. "I need to take care of my wife."

I bite back a moan, "I like that."

"What? When I call you my wife?" I nod, resting my head against his shoulder. "My wife."

"My husband," I whisper back, loving how the word rolls off my tongue. "Mine." I breathe as he kisses my neck, right beneath my ear.

"Yo Hudson, do you think we can be fed?" Jagger shouts, interrupting us.

"I should have put a bullet in him." He murmurs as I get off his lap and sit back down in my chair. He waves his hand and within seconds, the food is being brought to everyone.

I glance at Hudson and blow him a kiss as he winks at me, this right here is going to be one of the best memories I'll ever have. So much love and support under one roof and they're here for me and my husband.

TWELVE

Hudson

THE FILES TRANSFER from my computer to Mia's cell. As soon as we arrived back from the hotel this morning she asked me to copy them to her phone. She's currently sleeping, recovering from yesterday and last night. There's something very different about having her as my wife, something she felt last night, when I kept her awake most of the night. No matter how many times I had her, I needed her again, I couldn't get enough. Not only that, she couldn't get enough of me. I'd love nothing more than to go to bed and lie beside her but I can't. I have a meeting with Coby. He's late, that's just put me into a bad mood.

"Son?" Dad says knocking on my office door.

"Yeah?" I murmur distractedly as I finish off transferring the files.

"Where the hell is Coby?" He demands coming to sit down in front of me.

"Since when did I become his minder? I have no idea, he was due here ten minutes ago and he's not here. I'm giving him five more minutes before I lose my damn temper."

He chuckles, "You're in a good mood today."

I glare at him. "Is there a reason as to why you're here?"

The fucker chuckles yet again, "Yes, I wanted to know what Coby's going to do to help." I narrow my eyes at him and he holds his hands up. "Look son, Mia is my daughter now, she's carrying my grandchild. When you're gone I'll be the one to be here protecting her."

I shake my head. "You're a damn fool. Who else is going to be here with her when I'm gone? Since Mia and I got together, you've seemed to mellow. I actually can stand to be around you."

He laughs. "Yeah, since Mia came into your life you've not been such an asshole."

"Shut up old man, what's happening with you and mom?" Yesterday at the wedding they seemed to be getting along really well which is a huge fucking relief, I'm sick of their arguing.

"Your mom no longer wants to gut me while I sleep. She's got a new man and I'm happy for her." He smiles, it's a genuine one. "I have no idea who the man is, but he treats her wrong then he'll have the both of us to deal with."

I nod. "That he will. So how are you holding up?"

"I'm fine."

"Bullshit," I fire back, Mia told me about the conversation that he and Tina had the night before she died. He never mentioned anything to me about it, so I know that he's hurt even more about her dying. I thought it was over between them and now I find out that they had reconciled only for her to die the next day.

"Look son, there's nothing I can do about it. She's gone, I'm going to protect her daughter and our grandchild," he tells me, and I realize that's what is keeping him going.

A knock on my office door has both dad and I looking up. "Yeah?"

"Sorry I'm late." Coby's deep voice calls out, and the door opens. "Traffic is a fucking nightmare."

"Damn, you've been hitting those weights a bit hard," Dad says as he looks at the six-foot-five Coby, the man has bigger muscles than The Rock.

Coby ignores him and sits down beside him. "Any word on that asshole?"

"Nothing, he's in hiding," I say through clenched teeth, this should have never gotten this far.

Coby shakes his head. "After killing Tina and shooting your mom he ran like the fucking coward he is."

I don't need reminding of what he's done, I know everything, I found out things about him that I've not told anyone, sickening things that make me sick to my stomach. "We need to find him."

"You're going to have to tell me everything about him, I'll need to know all of his deepest darkest secrets." Coby says and I raise my brow in question. "You're telling me that you haven't delved into him since this shit has happened?" I glare at him and the fucker smiles. "Yeah, that's what I thought. Now, what did you find out?"

"Martin prefers brunettes, the younger they are the better." I inform them.

Dad's eyes narrow. "How young exactly?"

"In the past six weeks, I've had twelve men come to me, these men aren't mine, they're not even in our circle. They know me, they know what I do and they knew Martin was my man. They told me that Martin had sex with their daughters and when the parents found out he told them that they'd have me to deal with." I say with disgust, each one of those men had the courage to face me, to explain what that fucker did to their daughters.

"How old were they?" Dad bites out.

"They range in age from thirteen to sixteen."

Dad jumps to his feet, "That animal has been raping these young girls and putting the fear into their parents." He shakes his head. "Everything about him makes me sick."

"We all know there's something wrong with the man, but from everything I've heard, it seems as though he wants revenge." Coby says and I smile as he glares at dad, Coby doesn't give a shit, he says whatever he wants and doesn't care about the consequences. "Harrison, you abandoned him, you favored Hudson over him and he wants revenge for that."

Dad sits back down again, he's resigned, he knows what Coby is saying is true. "Okay, what is he going to do next?"

"I believe that he's not finished, he tried to kill Marline and he failed, so he could try again. I'd up security on both Marline and Mia, if he wants revenge, that's where I'd start. I think his end game will be killing everyone Harrison loves, including Hudson. He may even kill you Harrison."

"That's not going to happen." I vow, "It's why I've asked for your help. I need to find that fucker before he hurts anyone else."

"Son…" Dad begins, "this isn't your fault."

"Yes, Dad, it is. I should have seen who he was. I shouldn't have let him get that close to me."

Dad's eyes shutter close. "If it's anyone's fault, it's mine."

"You should have told me who Martin was, if you had I would have never let him climb the ranks. Saying that, I'm the boss, I should have seen who he was. We've all let him get close and that has been to our detriment. Now it's time to end him."

Coby smiles, "That's what I'm here for. I never did like that jackass. Now, I have a friend who may be able to help us. There's a network for people like Martin that like young girls or boys. My friend is undercover and has managed to infiltrate that network. I'm going to reach out and see if he knows Martin, it could help us find him if he does."

Fucking hell, if I was undercover I'd kill every single fucker that was part of that network, there's no way I'd be able to act as though I was friends with one of them. Fucking sick bastards. There's no way I could listen to the shit they'd say. "Do it." I tell Coby, the sooner he makes contact the better.

He gets to his feet, pulling his cell out of his pocket and makes his way out of the office.

"Son, I owe you an apology. I should have told you about Martin."

"Yes dad, you should have." I'm not going to lie to him, he fucked up.

"Your grandfather and I argued up until the day he died over it too. I told him that he shouldn't have brought him into the family, your grandfather thought otherwise. Had he known the shit he was bringing into our lives he'd have done it differently."

I sigh. "That may be so Dad, but I still don't know why you didn't tell me, I mean you made him my chauffeur and bodyguard. Don't you think that was rubbing it in his face a bit?"

"Hindsight is a strange thing. Yes, I regret putting him as your bodyguard. I thought having him do that would keep him out of my business."

"There's nothing we can do about it now, what's done is done. Why did you tell my mom about him?" I'm curious, Mom claims that Dad never loved her, but he told her about Martin, which says otherwise.

"Your mom and I had a weird relationship. As I've said, I've made a lot of mistakes, more with your mom than anyone else. Your mom thought our marriage was based on love, whereas I always thought of it as a convenience, your mom knew about our lifestyle, she knew the rules and obeyed them. I should have made it more clear to her about what I felt and what I wanted from the marriage."

"So why did you tell her?" I ask again, my dad would make a great politician, he dodges questions like a pro.

He sighs heavily. "Your mom made me promise at the beginning that there would be no secrets between us. I told her about Martin along with every other stupid mistake I made while I was young."

"So what changed, when did you stop being honest and faithful?" I'm fucking glad that I found Mia, I wouldn't bring myself to marry someone I don't love. Hell I definitely wouldn't have had children with them.

"Your mom and I argued a lot, she knew that I didn't love her, I never told her I did, I wouldn't do that. She hated me for not loving her and I resented her for falling in love with me. The arguments turned violent and we're both at fault for it. I should never have laid my hands on her but your mom gave as good as she got. I'm not justifying what I did, but giving you the entire story. You hated me because you thought I was a liar and a cheater. Your mom married me knowing that I didn't love her and that I was with other women."

Fuck, I didn't want to know this shit, "Yes dad, I get that but you still treated her like crap, you made her cry every day."

He turns away from me, "I know that, but what was I

supposed to do? Pretend that I loved her? I wasn't lying to her, I never lied to her."

"Dad, you beat her until she was bloody," I say through clenched teeth, the memory of her lying on the floor with blood over her face, a tooth missing, and a swollen eye.

Guilt is written all over his face. "I know, and that was the last time I ever raised my hand to her. I went too far that day, I knew that it was time to leave. Things between us got real bad, I left and went to Tina as I knew that it would be the only way we could move on. I never intended on divorcing your mom that was never on the cards. Until that day, I lost it, I couldn't take the arguments, the shouting, the threats."

I change the subject, nothing good can come from this. What dad's saying makes me doubt everything mom has told me. Yes dad was violent, a cheater, and he was angry, but what he's told me is mom knew about Tina and by the sounds of it, others. Their marriage wasn't what she made out. I'm not going to delve into it any deeper. Right now, I get along with both of my parents and if I find out mom lied, I'm going to be pissed. "Dad, are you going to be able to kill Martin if the time comes?" It's something I've been unsure of, even though he says he hates him, I'm not sure if he'd be able to kill his son.

"Yes," he says without hesitation. "I understand where that question has come from, but my loyalty is to you, not only as the boss but because you are my son."

I raise my brow. "He is your son too!"

He's shaking his head, "No, he isn't. Having sex with his mom was stupid, I told her to get a damn abortion but she didn't listen. She thought that she would trap me by keeping it. Stupid fucking decision ever. She ended up crawling back to her husband and acting as though it was his. I never had anything to do with any of them again, until Martin began acting out, your grandfather thought he'd step in and help. Even when Martin joined our organization, I made sure that he was kept away from me. So no, I won't have any qualms about killing him. He is not my son, never was and never will be. That fucker killed my wife and raped my daughter. He's a dead man."

That makes sense in such a fucked up way. "Good, because I don't want you to go crazy when I kill that fucking asshole."

"You have no worries," Dad reiterates and relief washes through me. I believe him, he's not going to stop me nor is he going to give a shit.

The office door opens and Coby walks back in. "Spoke to my friend," he says with a smile as he sits down. "Now my friend is a cop but he also knows me and knows about you."

I cross my arms over my chest, glaring at him.

He tuts. "Not in that way asshole, I wouldn't do that. I meant he knows what you both did for me and he's going to help us out. Martin is part of that network. He's reached out in the last couple of weeks, he's been using his contacts to stay hidden. Martin has given my friend all the information he needed to find out where they hide when the cops are looking for them. They help one another out so they're not found."

I shake my head in disgust, fucking sick bastards. "Where is he?"

Coby's smile widens. "I know where he'll be tomorrow. He's coming back, he'll be staying in Long Beach."

"How accurate is this intel?" I question.

"Highly. These men and women are extremely cautious. They only trust each other, there's no way he's going to believe anyone will know where he is. They communicate via the dark web, no one can infiltrate it or so they think. It's got a high level security and only members can access the site, there's only one way you can become a member and that's if you are invited."

Fucking hell. "You'd think they're running some sort of military op or some shit."

Coby nods. "Close enough, the man that set the site up is a military man."

"Fucking sick fucks." Dad growls in disgust. "We'll have the fucker surrounded, he won't know what hit him."

"We need to coordinate with my friend, once you take Martin down, the others are going to scramble. So we need to time it perfectly so that no one gets spooked," Coby tells us.

"We'll arrange it for early in the morning. We'll have him being watched, but that way, he'll believe that he's fine where he is."

"Hudson, that's good, it'll give him a false sense of security along with making the others relax. Getting them early in the morning or late at night will mean they're asleep and won't be expecting it," Coby says. "Let me know the time and I'll have my friend coordinate it with his task force."

"Four am, arrange it and let me know, then we're going to set up surveillance, I want my men there as soon as possible in case he turns up early."

Coby gets to his feet, a smile on his face and his cell to his ear as he leaves my office.

"Not long left son, we're going to get him. The walls are closing in."

I smirk. "That fucker is going to be in a world of pain when I get my hands on him."

"Payback's a bitch." Dad smiles, baring his teeth.

"Dad, find a quiet place for us to bring him. Somewhere no one will stumble upon us or hear his tortured screams."

Dad gets to his feet. "I have the perfect place. I'll have it ready for you. We're going to get him son, we're going to make sure he knows that he's messed with the wrong fucking people." Dad leaves and I get to my feet, I'm looking forward to seeing Mia's face when I let her know that Martin is dead. That the monster is gone.

THIRTEEN

Mia

"MIA, ARE YOU OKAY?" Sarah's voice pulls me from my inner musings.

Blinking, I look at her, "Huh?"

She tilts her head to the side, studying me carefully. "Mia, you've been quiet, are you okay?"

Glancing at Hudson's closed office door I sigh. "Today was one of the best days I've had in a long time, we're all so happy. I was so stupid, I stopped looking over my shoulder. Martin has been quiet for so long, I was naive thinking that it was over."

She grasps my hand. "We all did, we all thought he'd given up. I truly believed that this was over. You're not naive, just as I'm not. He played us, we all had our guards down, but Mia, we're not sure if their meeting is about Martin."

I roll my eyes. "God, this is so fucked up. I hate not knowing what's happening."

She gives my hand a reassuring squeeze. "At least we got to shop." She smiles and I shake my head, she has her priorities right.

Hudson, Jagger, Harrison, Sarah, and I went shopping. We bought everything for our baby. We have his stroller, we bought his entire nursery furniture, and I couldn't help myself and bought loads of clothes for him. Once we'd finished shopping, we went for some lunch and that's when all hell broke loose. Hudson got a phone call, I watched as his eyes darkened and his jaw clenched. I knew immediately that something had happened, none of the men spoke. The entire car ride home was tense, and then as soon as we got home they went into his office and shut us out. They've been in there for almost three hours now and I've no idea what is happening. I'm scared, my mind instantly goes to Martin, wondering who he has hurt now, what has he done now?

"Jagger and I were talking…" She begins and I smile at her, "we really want to have Allie baptised, but not until Martin is gone. We want it to be a celebration, not have everyone looking over their shoulders."

"That sounds amazing, once all this is over, we're all going to be in need of a celebration."

Her smile widens. "We want both you and Hudson to be Allie's godparents."

Tears slowly fall down my face. "I'd be so honored to be Allie's godmother." Hudson and I have discussed who's going to be our baby's godparents and we want Sarah and Jagger to be them.

"There's no one in this world I'd want more. I love you. More than words can describe. You're someone that Allie will look up too, that will protect her."

"Always," I reply emphatically. I'd do anything for that little girl.

Sarah glances at her watch and then to Hudson's office door. "How much longer do you think they're going to be?"

I know that she's anxious, she wants to go back to Allie. Jagger's mom has her today, that woman absolutely adores her granddaughter. Whenever she can, she wants to be with her, it's something I absolutely love, I hope Marline is like that with our baby.

Grabbing my phone off the table I quickly send a text to Hudson asking him if he's okay. He doesn't respond and it hurts but there's nothing I can do about it. If he's not ready or not able to talk right now, then I'm going to have to wait. Until then, I'm going to have to make myself busy so that I don't go crazy. The thoughts are the worst, my mind is spinning with different scenarios, each one worse than the last.

I walk into the kitchen, I'm starting to get hungry and I know if I am, Hudson and Jagger are too. I chop garlic and coriander, I heat up butter over the stove and wait for it to melt, once it has, I add the garlic and coriander. I rub it under the skin of the chicken, it's something that Lacey taught me once, she said her grandmother showed her and it was the only meal she could cook. Once I have rubbed it into the chicken, I put the chicken into the oven and start peeling the potatoes and carrots. I can hear Sarah on the phone in the sitting room, she's checking up on Allie, she's been texting Jagger's mom all day.

I heat up a cooking tray with some Olive oil as my potatoes and carrots are boiling. Once the potatoes are par-boiled I put them into the heated tray and love hearing that sizzle as the olive oil hits them.

"Damn, something smells nice in here." I turn my head at that voice and smile. "You should be resting," Harrison tells me.

"I needed to keep busy, is your meeting finished?" I ask hopefully.

"Yeah, do you need any help?"

I shake my head. "No thank you. Grab a beer and take a load off. Dinner will be ready in thirty minutes."

He kisses my cheek. "Yell if you need a hand, I'll send Jagger in." He grabs a couple of beers from the fridge and I laugh, I can imagine him sending Jagger in here to help although if I really needed help, they'd all be here helping me.

Once Harrison leaves, I take out the potatoes out of the oven, placing the tray on top of the counter and turn the potatoes. They're crispy on the outside, just the way I wanted them to be. Once I put the tray back into the oven, I reach for the cupboard above my head and grab plates.

Hands slide around my waist and cup my bump, I smile as his head rests against my shoulder, his lips on my neck. "You okay, Princess?" he murmurs.

"Yeah," I lie. "Are you?" He makes a humming noise, I know that he's not, even though he's holding me he's still really tense. "Dinner's almost ready, will you set the table for me please?"

He places another kiss against my neck. "Of course." His hands withdraw from my stomach, and I instantly feel the loss. I bend down to take the chicken out of the oven, and jump when Hudson's voice booms. "What are you doing?"

Placing a hand on my chest, I turn to face him. "God, you scared the life out of me. I'm getting the chicken out of the oven, what does it look like?"

He glares at me, his jaw clenching. "Mia, you're six months pregnant, you shouldn't be bending over."

"Hudson, I am pregnant, not an invalid. I'm capable of bending over. Please just set the table." I feel as though he's scrutinizing every little thing I do. He's been checking up on seeing what a pregnant woman shouldn't be doing.

It's driving me crazy, I'm not stupid, I would never put my child at risk.

His face blanks, he knows that he's been annoying me by constantly saying things, it's as though he doesn't trust me or something and it's hurtful. I turn away from him and go back to doing what I was doing before he rudely interrupted me. He leaves the kitchen and I sigh with relief, we're not going to argue.

Once I have the dinner dished out, I bring it into the dining room. Everyone is sitting around the table waiting, the mood is tense and no one is talking. Placing the plates down in front of Hudson and Harrison, I don't say a word, I hate how awkward it is right now. I turn around and walk back into the kitchen, Sarah hot on my heels.

"They're all brooding assholes today. None of them have uttered a single word. They're so tense. I hate it," she tells me, her eyes so full of sadness. "I'm scared," she confesses.

"We're going to find out what the hell is going on." I'm not sitting in the dark, it's obvious that something has happened and I want to get to the bottom of it.

"Do you think they're going to say anything?" she asks as I hand her a plate.

I pick up the two remaining plates. "Hudson promised he wouldn't lie to me." I shrug, it's as simple as that.

Walking back into the dining room, the men are still wound up tight. I place a plate down in front of Jagger and walk to my seat.

"Thank you, Mia." Harrison says, Hudson and Jagger follow suit.

"You made Lacey's meal," Sarah whispers, her eyes glassy with unshed tears.

I smile at her, "Let's hope I do it justice." The men

stare at us with confusion. "Dig in," I tell them, and they instantly start to eat.

"This is so good," Sarah says as she eats. "Lacey would be so proud."

Tears well in my eyes, I really do hope that she would be. I miss her so much, she's always in my heart. She was like a sister to me, it's like there's a piece of my heart missing and I know that I'll never get it back.

"She's right, this is amazing. I didn't think you could cook," Hudson says with a smile.

"I can't really. I know how to cook some things. So, what happened today?" He glances at Jagger and it pisses me off, why can't he just say whatever the hell it is? "Hudson?"

"We finally figured out who Martin was getting his information from." His voice is cold and I'm actually beginning to worry.

"Who?" Sarah asks her gaze darting around the table.

"We're not sure if it was done deliberately or not," Jagger says but Harrison has a deep frown between his eyes, Hudson's focus is on his dinner.

"What the hell does that mean?"

"Remember when I said that mom must have been dating a new guy, because she came out of the funk she was in after dad did the shit he did?" Hudson asks and I nod, wondering where the hell he's going with this. "Well she and Martin had a thing."

My nose turns up in disgust, that's just nasty. "She told him everything?" I ask in disbelief.

Harrison lifts his beer to his lips, his eyes narrowing on Hudson.

"We're not sure what's happened, but it is possible that she told him stuff while they were together. The only way we're going to know for sure is to ask her." Hudson says and goes back to eating his dinner, that's his way of saying that the conversation is over.

"Wait, what?" Sarah asks, her eyes wide as she looks at Hudson. "You haven't asked her yet?"

"Sarah…" Jagger warns her.

"No, don't *Sarah* me anything. The man raped my best friend, he killed our friend, he killed her mom. He's killed your men. He has hurt Mia in ways no one is ever going to know and for what? Because he's under some delusion that he should be where Hudson is? He knew things about Mia, about our lives that he shouldn't have and you're telling me you found a connection but you're not doing anything about it."

"Sarah, this is his mom," Jagger tells her but I can see that he agrees with her.

"Fuck that, Mia is his wife, she is the mother of his unborn child. He should be finding out everything he can to ensure he finds that asshole. Not stepping on eggshells because it's his mom." She cries, tears running down her face. "By him not finding out just shows how little he cares about her."

Hudson doesn't respond, he keeps his head down and keeps eating.

I sigh, pushing my food around on my plate. So much for having a nice dinner. Sarah's right, he should be talking to his mom. He should be finding out what she told Martin and when. She could be the way to finding him. I don't understand why he wouldn't want to be questioning her. Something about this entire situation doesn't sit right with me.

Silence descends on the room, everyone is focused on eating, not one of us making eye contact with anyone. Hudson's head is practically buried in his plate, Harrison's eyes are narrowed as he glares at him. He's making it known that he doesn't agree with what Hudson's doing, I don't think anyone in this room is.

Once everyone is finished, I stand, I want some space to breathe. Right now, Hudson's being an asshole and everyone else is waiting for me to explode or something. I pick up everyone's plates and bring them to the kitchen. I'm currently in disbelief, I'm not sure if I can wrap my head around why he's not talking to Marline. One phone call is all that it'll take to clear this all up. I put the plates onto the counter, I'll rinse them and put them into the dishwasher.

"Mia?" Sarah's voice calls out and I turn to see both her and Jagger standing in the doorway to the kitchen. "We're going to leave now."

Jagger's arm goes around her shoulder and he pulls her into his body, he gives me a small smile, "Sorry to leave you in the middle of this shit storm."

I walk over to them and wrap my arms around Sarah, Jagger doesn't release her so the hug is awkward. "It's okay, I know how much Sarah's been missing Allie."

He laughs. "You have no idea, she has my mom harassed with all the messages."

Heat rises in Sarah's cheeks as she blushes. "I just worry, that's all."

I smile. "There's nothing wrong with that. Can you imagine what Hudson's going to be like once this baby is born?"

Sarah laughs, her eyes lighting up. "Oh he's going to make me look sane."

Jagger smirks. "I don't think that's possible," he mutters, quickly dodging Sarah's arm as it swings out to hit him.

"We're going before I kill him." She glares at Jagger. "I need snuggles with Allie."

I shoo them away. "Go, give Allie a kiss from me."

"Love you Mia, call me if you need me." She tells me planting a kiss on my cheek. I know what she means, if Hudson continues to be an asshole to call her she'll help calm me down.

"Love you too."

Jagger also kisses me on my cheek. "Thanks for dinner Mia, I really need to come here more often."

I shake my head as I roll my eyes. "Jagger, you're here more than anyone."

He glares at me. "And?"

Sarah drags him away. "Let's go before you annoy her. Talk to you later, Mia."

Once they walk away I turn back to do the dishes. My confusion of Hudson's decision is changing to anger. It seems as though he doesn't give a shit about me or our child.

"You okay, Mia?"

I jump at the voice, my heart pounds. God, he scared the crap out of me.

"Sorry, didn't mean to scare you," Harrison says as he reaches into the cupboard and takes down the bottle of Jack and a glass.

"It's okay, I was in a world of my own. I didn't hear you come in." I rinse off the plates and put them into the dishwasher.

"You doing okay?"

I shrug. "I guess."

"If anyone can get him to see sense it's you. Although Sarah sure gave him a lot to think about. Damn, that woman will give Jagger hell if he fucks up."

I smile. "Yes, there's no doubt about it."

"Just as you will. You two ladies are ferocious."

I turn to look at him. "We fight for what we want and

we protect those that we love. I also know the battles I need to fight and when to back off."

"And is this a battle you need to fight or back off from?" he asks with a raised brow.

"That, I'm not sure. I guess I'll find out once I talk to him."

He smiles at me. "Give him hell." He leaves the kitchen, and within moments I hear the front door close.

I finish the dishes, trying to tamper down my anger. I want to talk to him with a clear mind. God knows how that's going to work. My anger just seems to rise the longer we're apart. I'm pissed that he's putting our child's life in danger by not finding out all that he can.

FOURTEEN

Hudson

DOWNING THE GLASS OF JACK, I wait for the burn to come but it doesn't. Fucking useless. I'm angry, and this is doing nothing to help. I've spent the last hour getting my security updated and my protocols changed. While I was on the phone, I had more cameras added. The more eyes the better. The door to my office opens and I lift my head to see Mia walking into my office. She's not happy and I know why, hell I'm not fucking happy. This is a clusterfuck and I'm wondering just how I'm supposed to weave through the mess. She hesitates, then crosses her arms over her chest as she leans against the door.

"Are you ready to talk yet?" she asks me, her tone one of disappointment and I think I hear a hint of anger in there.

I sigh. "What do you want to talk about?" I ask deadpan and her eyes narrow at me. "Mia?" I question, I'm being an ass.

She raises her brow at me. "Hudson, I'm hormonal enough without having to deal with your stupidity. You know what I want to talk about. The fact that your mom could be the reason why Martin knows stuff he shouldn't."

I pour myself another drink, I knew that me trying to put her off wouldn't work. "Sit down, Princess." I tell her softly and immediately her stance changes, gone is the protective stance. She walks over to my desk, sitting down in front of me. "Thank you for dinner."

She glares at me, that's not what she was hoping to hear but it needed to be said. She spent a long time working on it and it went to fucking shit due to the bombshell that was dropped. "Hudson, why haven't you spoken to your mom?"

"I've tried. As soon as I found out, I texted her asking her to meet me here and she never responded. I've called her and I've had Aaron go to her place. She's not there."

Her eyes widen, her lips part in shock. "Where is she?"

"I have no idea, I have my men looking for her."

Her mouth opens and quickly closes again. "Do you think she's with Martin?" Her body shakes as she says his name.

My hand grasps my glass and I bring it to my lips, I empty the contents with one swallow. "No. Mia, there's no way that my mom has done this."

She glances away from me. "How certain are you?"

I narrow my eyes. "Mia, this is my mom."

She looks at me as if she's never seen me before. "Look, I'm not saying she's done anything wrong. But Hudson, if she's been seeing him in a romantic way, she could have accidentally let things slip, she could be with him now."

"For fuck sake, Mia, there's no way."

She shakes her head and gets to her feet. "I'm glad you're certain. But I'm not. Everything that has happened, screams that someone has been helping him. I'm disappointed that you'd put our child at risk by not asking her a simple question."

I slam my hands down on my desk and get to my feet. Mia jumps, fear creeping into her eyes. "How can you say that?" I bite out. "That is my child Mia, mine. I'll do everything in my power to protect it."

"Then fucking ask her the damn question Hudson," she screams at me, her hands waving in the air. Tears begin to trickle down her face. "How hard is it? Hmm? To ask a question?"

"My mom wouldn't do this."

She takes a step backward, her head shaking in disgust. "I'm done," she tells me and walks out of my office.

A red haze forms and I go blank. Done? What the hell does she mean by done? "Done?" I roar stalking after her. My hand grips her arm and I pull her to a stop, her body slamming against mine. "Done?" I ask her once again, my face mere inches from hers.

"Done, Hudson. I'm done with this conversation. What's the point in talking when you obviously don't give a crap about me or my feelings." Her tears are falling thick and fast and I fucking hate that I'm making her cry. "You're so certain and yet you didn't think Martin would have betrayed you either. You need to open your eyes Hudson, how many times are people I love going to get hurt? How many more people am I going to lose because you're a stubborn asshole?" She's lashing out now, I'm taking those blows, I deserve to take them. Everything she's saying is right, because of me she's been hurting.

I lift my hands and frame her face. "Mia, you're fucking all I think about. You matter."

She blinks, not believing what I'm saying.

I wipe away her tears with my thumb. "You're everything, Mia, you and our child come first. Always."

"Okay," she whispers but she doesn't sound convinced. She's pissed and I understand why. "What now?"

I caress her face. "Now I talk to my mom, find out if she's behind this."

Her eyes widen. "Really?"

Fuck, does she think I'm that much of an asshole? Not to her, she's the only one that doesn't see that side of me, or so I thought.

"Yes, Princess, really. The stress is something you don't need."

She shakes her head. "When you didn't talk to me that stressed me out."

I pull her closer to me. "Sorry, baby." I'm a fucking asshole.

"It's okay, how are you feeling?" she asks me, her hands running up and down my back.

"My head's fucking spinning. If what we found out is true then I'm going to fucking go crazy."

"If she has told him stuff, I don't think she did it on purpose."

I roll my eyes. "Mia, she would have still told him."

Pulling away from me she sighs. "Think about it, when you're in love with someone you talk about everything. Your mom could have told him in confidence. Depending when things were said obviously, but don't go too hard on her."

"We'll see, now we just have to wait until my men find her."

She tilts her head and stares at me. "What if he has her?"

"We're going to find her, don't worry." I reassure her but I'm not so fucking sure, the shit that Martin has done in the past has me on edge.

"I know you will." She yawns, and I realize just how

tired she is, her eyelids heavy, I'm taking most of her weight. "Sorry," she says sheepishly.

I lift her into my arms. "Don't apologize, my boy's taking it out of you. You overdid it today." She rests her head on my shoulder. "Want to have a bath or go straight to bed?"

"Bed," she whispers, her lips grazing my skin at my neck.

I walk to the bedroom with her in my arms, she's fast asleep before I even place her on the bed. I take her clothes off so that she'll be comfortable while she's sleeping. Once I have her all stripped down, I pull the covers over her. She immediately curls up into them, her hair spread over the pillow. She looks at peace, something that I know she hasn't felt in a long time. I stand here and stare at her, God, she's gorgeous, I'm one lucky sonofabitch. I don't know what I've done to deserve her, but I'm holding on with both hands.

Now this shit with my mom, I still can't fucking comprehend how the hell this happened? Dad's fucking pissed, his ex-wife sleeping with his son. It's a messed up situation and he's wondering just how long it had been going on for. I want to know if it's still going on. The sooner my men find her the better, I'm an impatient man and I hate waiting. The front door opens and I know that it's Dad, he left to give Mia and I space, he told me I'd fucked up and needed to fix it. He has a soft spot for Mia, it's why I leave him with her if I need to go out. He'll protect her with his life.

I walk out of the bedroom and meet dad in the sitting room, his jaw's clenched and I brace myself to see what's to come. "The boys have your mom."

I tilt my head to the side as I study him, his lips

thinned, his arms hanging down by his sides and his fists are clenched. "And?"

He shakes his head. "Prepare yourself son, that bitch has taken everyone for a fucking fool."

Red hot anger hits me. "Dad!"

He waves me off. "Son, she was with him." Anger pouring off every inch of him. "She has no injuries, she was pissed when we arrived."

I swallow harshly. "She was with him willingly?" I don't even recognize my own voice right now. For the first time in my life, I'm fucking shocked.

He nods, his eyes narrowing. "She didn't want to leave him."

"They have him?"

Dad laughs. "No, that weasel ran as soon as the men rolled up."

I look to the floor, I'm mad as hell, Dad was right, she has been helping him. I'm angry that she's the reason my wife has been in so much fucking pain. She's the reason why my dad lost the love of his life.

"Son," Dad chokes and I glance at him, his eyes glassy. "There's something that doesn't make sense. When Tina was shot, so was your mom, why would she go back to him when he shot her?"

I have no fucking idea. "I'm going to find out. Who's watching her?"

He takes a seat. "Aaron, David, and Rory. I've got Mia, go find out what the fuck is going on."

I should grab my keys and go, but I hesitate, there's something in my gut that's telling me not to leave.

Dad must sense my hesitance. "Son, I've got her, there's no way I'd let anything happen to her. She's safe with me."

"I know that. You're one of the very few that I trust to

keep her safe. My gut's screaming." I admit feeling like an asshole leaving her but right now, I have to find out this shit.

"Your gut is never wrong." He tells me as he takes out his cell. "Get three of your men here." His cell buzzes. "Coby's still in town, he'll be here in ten."

Relief washes through me, at least she'll be protected if anything does happen. "Thanks. Call Jagger, get his ass here too." I pull out my cell and text Dylan, Roland, and Cormac. Those men have shown their loyalty and I somewhat trust them. I tell them they have fifteen minutes to get here. I don't give a fuck what they're doing, they'll drop everything or I'll drop them.

"Jagger's on his way, he'll be here in a few minutes," Dad tells me, "Are you going to wake Mia and let her know that you're leaving?"

"Yeah, Dylan, Roland, and Cormac should be here within fifteen minutes. Once they're here I'm leaving. I'm going to find out what the fuck is going on and then get back here." I'm hoping this shit will be over within an hour.

"Son, we have her covered. Find out this shit and we can end it."

I turn on my heel and walk out of the sitting room and into our bedroom. Mia's sitting up in bed, her gaze firmly on me. "They've found your mom."

I nod. "The men are on their way, I want to make sure you're safe while I'm gone."

"Can I come with you?" she whispers.

I walk toward her. "No Mia, I need you to stay here." I'm about to turn into a monster and she doesn't need to see that shit, she doesn't need to be in that situation. She's safest here. I sit down on the bed beside her. "Dad's here, Coby and Jagger are on their way."

She glances away from me, she's not happy at all. "Okay."

"Mia, I need you safe and that's you being here."

She turns back to face me. "I know," she confesses quietly, "I'm scared, Hudson, I can't lose you." Tears fall down her face.

Fuck, I pull her closer to me. "Princess, I'm going to be okay. I'm just going to have a conversation with my mom and then I'm coming home."

She nods. "Be safe."

"Always." I kiss her lips. "Are you going back to sleep?"

She frowns. "No, I'm going to get dressed and sit with your dad."

I hide my smile, she's about to make my dad's night. I know that when those two are together they talk about Tina. It's her way of being close to her mom. I never thought my dad would be this involved in my life, but things have changed, he has changed. The way he treats my wife, he's turned into a man I respect.

I wait with her while she gets dressed. "Mia, if anything happens tonight. I need you to go into my office and lock yourself in there."

Her eyes widen but she nods immediately. "I will, I promise."

"In the top drawer is a gun, there's also a knife tapped under the desk."

"Hudson," she whispers, her entire body shaking.

"Mia, listen to me. If anything happens, go there, get a weapon and fight. This place is wired to the max. Something happens, I'm going to know about it. I'll be here within minutes," I promise her.

She walks over to me, her hands sliding around my waist. "Okay, but we're going to be fine. You're going to talk to your mom and you're coming home," she tells me mimicking my own words from earlier.

I kiss her nose. "That's exactly it, Princess."

There's a knock at the door and dad yells, "I'll get it."

"They're here. It's time to go." I take her hand, she interlocks her fingers with mine.

When we get to the sitting room, I see that everyone except Jagger is here. "Dylan, Cormac, Ronald, and Coby you are to be posted outside." They instantly nod. "Once Jagger gets here, he will be posted inside of the house. Kill anyone who tries to come in."

I kiss Mia once again and say goodbye, I need to get out of here before I change my damn mind and send dad to deal with mom. The men instantly follow me outside, as I slide into my car, they position themselves outside. Each one of them strapped and ready to go, Coby will take the lead, the man knows tactics and knows the best way to react. He'll size up my men and instantly pinpoint their weaknesses along with their strengths and he'll play on them.

WALKING INTO MY CLUB, I IGNORE THE SHOCKED LOOK OF my bar staff. I've not been here in a while. It's still not reopened yet. My staff are working hard to have it ready for reopening next week. We're doing a big fucking relaunch, the place looks good. I have had it extended, the fire damage wasn't as bad as it could have been but it did need a makeover. Pushing the door open that leads to the cellar, I hear Mom shouting. "Let me the fuck out of here."

I walk down the stairs and see that David's sitting down on the chair glaring at Mom. I'm guessing the reason

David lost his wife is because of mom. I'm surprised that he's not made her bleed. I'm not sure I'd have that much restraint if it were me in his position.

Mom sighs, "Finally. Hudson, what the hell is going on? Why am I here? Your goons haven't said anything, they grabbed me and brought me here."

"Where did they grab you from?" I say through clenched teeth. There's no being nice now, she's acting as though she's done nothing wrong, we all know where she was taken from.

Her eyes widen. "What?" she questions glancing around the room.

"I said, where did my men take you from?"

She straightens her spine. "You already know, what I want to know is why they took me in the first place." She raises her brow at me as though I should answer her questions.

I smirk. "This doesn't work like that. You don't get to ask me questions. Not when you've been sleeping with that asshole."

She's unable to mask the shock on her face. "How?"

"How did I find out?" She nods. "My men have been searching through Martin's records. His bank accounts, his cell records, I know every little thing about him. So imagine my surprise when I find loads of calls and texts to your number. Your face on security feeds on hotel getaways you two have been on. So how long, Mom? How long has this been going on?"

She glances away unable to look me in the eye. "A while."

"That's not an answer Mom. How long?"

"Five years." she whispers, turning back to face me.

I glare at her. "Five years? You made out as though Dad was the one that ended your marriage. You played the innocent victim, when you were the one that was cheating." Disgust laces each and every word I say.

"No, your father was an asshole. He didn't care about me, he drove me into Martin's arms."

"Into the arms of his son?"

Her eyes flash with anger. "I love him."

I laugh. "You've given him everything he could have needed to bring me down. Tell me something, who shot you?"

She narrows her eyes at me. "Martin did."

"So you love him but he obviously doesn't love you." Her eyes are almost slits now. "You don't shoot the woman you love."

"If he wanted to kill me, he could have done it."

I ignore her stupid fucking comment. "You went to him willingly today?"

"Yes," she bites out.

"Where is he now?" She glances away, fuck, she knows exactly where he is. "Mom, what the fuck is wrong with you? He's hurt Mia, he fucking raped her and you're helping him? You're still fucking him?" I'm utterly disgusted, this is not the woman that raised me.

"He said he didn't, that it wasn't him."

"Are you for fucking real? Mom, the asshole gave her a gift when he found out she was pregnant. He thought my son was his." I walk up to her. "What the fuck happened to you? My mom would never allow someone to manipulate her the way he is doing."

She looks me dead in the eye. "Your father broke me."

"Bullshit," I fire back. "You gave Dad as good as you got. Yes, he was an asshole and he did things he shouldn't have, but you never once backed down. If it were dad doing this, there's no way you'd be sticking up for him the way you are for Martin."

Her lip trembles, I've hit a nerve. "What do you want, Hudson?"

I glance at David, he's shaking his head, when I turn to Aaron he looks as though he wants to kill her. "Mom, take a look around this room." She lifts her head and looks at them both. "Martin has killed innocent women, he has killed my men, he burned Aaron. You sit there and act as though Martin is a fucking saint. You're crazy."

"You want me to give him up so that you can kill him."

"It's either kill him or him kill us. So yeah, when I get my hands on him I'm going to kill him, I'm going to make sure that he's out of our lives forever. So that he won't be able to hurt my child."

"He's at…."

She's cut off with my phone beeping like crazy. My blood runs cold. That beep tells me that someone's at my house. Taking my cell out of my pocket, I tap on the alarm. It instantly brings up footage from my house. My feet are moving as I see Coby lying on the ground outside the house. Fuck. Swiping to the right, it changes to the feed inside of the house. Martin has his gun pointed at Dad.

Fuck! Fuck! Fuck!

Where's Mia?

FIFTEEN

Mia

"YOU'VE NEVER TOLD me what your favorite memory was." I pull the blanket up over my legs and settle in to hear his story. He always has a story to tell me, something that's bound to make me smile.

His eyes light up, "The day we got married. Your mom looked amazing. She shone with happiness. While we married alone, you and Hudson weren't far from our thoughts. She was a true vision as she walked down the aisle toward me. I knew in that moment that I was going to spend the rest of my life with her."

"I saw the pictures, she really looked amazing. I don't think I ever saw her as happy as those few weeks I spent with the two of you." Even when she felt as though she was losing me, she was still happy with Harrison.

"Your mom wanted the best for you and she knew you were happy with Hudson, that he was the man to make you happy and love you like no other. She also knew that being with him would put you in grave danger, and it has." He reaches for his bottle of beer, he brings it to his lips and takes a long sip. "But what your mom soon realized once we got you back was it wasn't Hudson that put you in that danger, it was me. Who I am, what I did. She understood that no matter what happened, Hudson would do anything in his power to ensure your safety. It was then she realized that she was only hurting herself by trying to separate the two of you."

"By then it was too late."

He nods. "Yes, she never got to talk to you properly, but you heard her words and I know that they meant a lot to you. That would have been her biggest regret not apologizing to you both."

"I knew she loved me, I just couldn't understand the hatred."

His eyes fill with sadness "It wasn't hatred, it was confusion and jealousy. She couldn't understand why you wouldn't listen to her. You had grown up so much and she was jealous that you no longer needed her. It hurt her that she had lost so much time with you."

I blink back my tears, "We both messed up. I have so many regrets when it comes to her and our relationship."

"We all do, Mia, it's what happens when someone is taken from us too early. We look back on things and see what we should have done differently. We use those mistakes to ensure we never make them with another loved one." I guess that's why he's so determined to make amends with Hudson.

"What do you think is happening with Marline?" I haven't been able to stop thinking about it since Hudson's left.

Harrison's jaw clenches. "If it were up to me, I'd have her killed." I suck in a sharp breath, he wouldn't really kill his mom, would he? "But it's not, it's up to Hudson. There's no way he'd do that to her. He'll buy her stupid sob story."

I knew that they hated each other, but his attitude is so cold toward her. "Don't you believe that she was led on? Used to gain information?"

He laughs. "Marline led on? Used? No, Mia, I don't believe it. Marline is the manipulator, she can turn every single situation around so that she looks like a victim. I laid my hands on her in anger twice. It was wrong and it was the reason why I left her, not your mom, but because together we were toxic."

"That's exactly how Hudson described your marriage."

His smile is a sad one, he closes his eyes as if he's in pain. "No child should ever see their parents as toxic. Marline turned my boy against me from a young age, I should have nipped that shit in the bud but I didn't and that's on me. She learned how to manipulate people from the get-go and hasn't stopped."

I'm shocked, Marline doesn't come across that way.

"Mia, don't be surprised if she's been pulling his strings," Harrison tells me, his eyes dark with rage.

I gasp, there's absolutely no way that Hudson's mom would ever hurt him like that. She knows everything that Hudson's been through. "She wouldn't do that to Hudson."

"We'll have to wait for Hudson to get back."

"But, if she's as manipulative as you say, he won't see it."

He shakes his head. "No, when Hudson left here this evening, he was determined to get the truth. He's not going to let her manipulate him."

I'm glad that Harrison's so sure about it because I'm not. I have no idea what to think, I'm utterly confused as to what's going on. I'm doubting everything I ever thought about Marline and I don't even know if she's guilty of passing on information to Martin.

The fine hairs on the back of my neck stand up as a shrill beeping fills the air. Harrison's up on his feet with a gun in his hand within seconds. "Mia, Hudson told you what to do. Do it," he instructs, his eyes on me, pleading with me to do as he says.

I'm frozen to the spot when gunshots ring out.

"Mia go. Now," he yells at me.

My feet take me to Hudson's office, as I place my hand on the door handle, I turn to see Harrison staring at me. I don't want to leave him but I know that I need to. "Be safe," I tell him and walk into the office.

As soon as I lock the door behind me, I run behind his desk. I fumble with the drawer, Hudson told me to get the gun. As soon as my hand grips the butt, I pull it from the drawer and crawl under the desk. My entire body is shaking, but I do as Hudson tells me and take the knife that's taped under the desk and grip it in my hand.

"Where is she?" I whimper at that voice, it's so full of rage.

"She's not here. You're not going to find her," Harrison tells him and I scoot further under the desk and bring my knees to my chest. *God, please Hudson, come home.*

"She's carrying my child. You can't hide her from me."

Harrison's laugh is sarcastic and I cringe, he's going to make things worse. "She's not carrying your baby. Even if she were, do you honestly believe that we'd let you anywhere near her?"

"So she is having my baby," My eyes widen at Martin's words.

"No, you fucking moron, she's carrying Hudson's baby." Harrison's really not making things any better.

"Where is she?" he asks once again.

My heart's beating faster than ever before. I won't let him take me this time. Never again.

"Martin, Mia isn't the one you want. Hell, Hudson's not the one you're angry with." Harrison's voice has lost that edge to it, his tone very similar to the one that he uses with Hudson.

"Yes, I am fucking angry with Hudson. He's taken everything that should have been mine, including my baby." Martin isn't calming down, he seems to get more agitated with every word that Harrison says.

"No, he hasn't, Mia was pregnant when you took her. You kidnapped and raped a pregnant woman." Harrison has a bite to his tone. "Martin, you hurt her. Why?"

"Why?" he asks incredulously. "Because she was his."

"Is, not was. She is Hudson's, she's his wife, the mother of his child. Mia is the love of his life. He had no idea who you were to him, and yet he treated you like a brother. What did Hudson ever do to deserve everything you've done to him?"

Oh God, why is Harrison asking this? He should have waited until help had got here. Anything could make Martin kill him, I can't lose someone else I care about, I've already lost so much.

"He has everything, I have nothing."

"Bullshit." I close my eyes, not wanting to hear anymore, it's as though he's taunting Martin. "You had your parents, you had this family, you had everything you ever wanted."

"I never had you." Martin screams and my heart breaks for him. "You never wanted me. Henry told me, he said he was the reason that I was brought into the fold, not because you wanted me but because he wanted me." His voice is small, he reminds me of a little boy who's lost. Right now, I can't help but feel for him. It must have been hard for him to be around Harrison and not have the relationship that most fathers and sons have.

"No, you never had me. I was young and stupid when your mom and I had an affair. She returned to her life, married your father and I returned to mine and this organization. You had a family, why the fuck are you pissed that I never wanted you? Have you not seen my life? How fucked up it is?"

"You are my father and you acted to the entire world as though I was nothing but a fucking grunt. You and Hudson expect the utmost respect and yet you couldn't pay me the same. I am entitled to the respect that you both have. I have the Brady blood running through my veins."

Harrison laughs and I cringe. "You think it's the Brady name that means you deserve respect? You think that because Hudson is my son that's why he gets the respect? Hudson earned his respect before he became boss, he earned the respect of those around him by the way he carried himself, by protecting me, protecting my men. You were there, you witnessed him putting a bullet in Jonathan's head when he pulled a gun on me. Hudson was fifteen and he was the quickest to his gun, quickest to react."

"So fucking what? Anyone could have done that." He sounds bitter and this conversation is getting them nowhere, Harrison isn't going to act any differently toward him.

"Hudson doesn't just have the respect of his men, he has the respect of the majority of players in this fucking country. Hudson is the boss, not because of who I am but because of who he is. He is a fucking gentleman, he'd never betray anyone, and he certainly wouldn't rape anyone." Harrison yells at him and I shrink even further into the desk. "You aren't mad at Hudson, you're jealous.

You're fucking angry with me because I didn't want you. Had Hudson known who you were, things could have been different between you. You would never have been boss, you would never have been given the respect."

"Why?" Martin questions and I'm scared, as I have no idea what the answer is going to be.

"You are my illegitimate child. A bastard if you will. My men would have never accepted you."

I shake my head. That is an awful thing to say, tonight I have heard the ugly side to Harrison and I'm not sure I'll ever be able to not hear what he's said.

A gunshot rings out and I squeak, fear rises through me. Who fired the shot? Is Harrison okay? My hand tightens on the gun as I focus my breathing so that I can hear. It's silent, I have no idea what has happened.

"Oh Mia...." Martin taunts.

Tears slide down my face, he's going to find me.

"I know you're here. Too many men for you not to be. I'm going to find you." He sings and I bite back another whimper. "That asshole is bleeding like the pig he is." He lets out a maniacal laugh. "It's just a matter of time before he bleeds out. You have a choice Mia, you either come out and save him, or you stay hidden and have his death on your conscious."

"No Mia. don't do it!" Harrison calls out. He's in pain, I can tell by his strained voice.

Martin laughs again. I hate that sound, it sends chills throughout my entire body. "Well look at him playing step-daddy dearest. We all know where his loyalties lie."

I bite back the scream not wanting him to know where I am, when another gunshot rings out. God, why is he doing this? He's already caused enough pain, this is just overkill.

"Oh, Mia, Mia, Mia you're hiding away like a scared

jackrabbit. What am I going to do with you?" He's taunting me, he's not going to stop, not until he has me.

I hear Harrison groaning and every instinct inside of me tells me to leave this hiding place and go out and face Martin so that Harrison can get help. I also know that Martin has killed people for doing less than what Harrison's done to him. There's a chance that even if I were to go out there, Martin would still kill him.

"Leave her alone." Harrison's voice isn't as strong as it was.

I need to get out there, I have to try and save him. Crawling out from under the desk, I look down at the gun and knife in my hands. If I go out there and he sees them, he'll be even angrier. I quickly put the gun into the band of my sweatpants and the knife into my pocket. I take a couple of deep breaths before I even turn to go to the door. I'm not ready for this, I'm not ready to face him, not again. But for Harrison, I have to. He'd do anything to protect me and right now, it's my turn to do the same for him.

The office door splinters open and I turn in shock. Martin's standing there with a sinister smile on his face. "You've gotten bigger since the last time I saw you." His eyes rake over my body, lust burning brightly in those green eyes of his.

I shudder in repulsion. "Martin." I whisper horrified as I'm staring face to face with the monster who haunts my dreams.

He takes a step into the office and I take two backward. "I've missed you," he tells me, that stupid smile on his face.

I bite back a whimper as he takes another step into the room. "What do you want?" I'm surprised at how strong my voice is, I'm a mess on the inside but at least he can't see that.

He tilts his head as if he's studying me. "That's not what I expected."

"What?"

He licks his lips. "I was told that you were broken."

I don't know why but hearing him say those words pisses me off. "Well whoever told you that got it wrong. You never broke me, you never had the power." It's true, he never did have the power to do that to me. He hurt me, in ways I don't think he'll ever comprehend. But he didn't break me and he never will. The only person who has the power is Hudson, looking at Martin now just proves that he has no hold over me.

He smiles wider. "You're making things much more tempting." His eyes once again rake over my body. "What we did before, we're going to do again. I don't give a fuck what Harrison says, that baby is mine, you know it and I know it. What I don't understand is why are you pretending otherwise?"

I look at him in disgust. "My baby isn't yours!" I shout, annoyed that he's still saying that. "What Harrison says is true. I was pregnant before you kidnapped me. There is no way this baby is yours. But let me make one thing extremely clear, even if this baby was yours, there is no way on God's green earth that I would let you anywhere near him. Finding out that Hudson was my baby's dad was the happiest day of my life. Knowing that you had no part in this child's life is a blessing."

His eyes flash with anger. "You're a bitch. I should have killed you when I had the chance. Maybe Lacey would be more pliable? Hell maybe your mum would have been better?" His mouth twists into a grin. "That has to be the sweetest killing of them all."

Pain stings my heart at his words. I want to bring my hand up and rub it away but I won't give him the satisfaction of knowing his words hurt. "Why did you kill my mom?" It's something I wanted to know, it's been on my mind since it's happened

He shrugs, not caring one bit about what he's done. "Your mom meant the most to Harrison, beside Hudson obviously. It was the most obvious choice to deal the most pain."

He's evil. "You wanted to hurt Harrison so much that you don't think of anyone else. You killed the only family I had left. You murdered my mom for what? Revenge?" Tears sting my eyes, I will them with all my might not to fall. Not to let him know that he's getting to me. "You wanted to cause Harrison the most pain. You didn't, you hurt me the most. Hell, you killing my mom hurt me more than you did when you raped me."

His eyes narrow, and I swear I see a tiny bit of remorse, but as quick as it comes, it disappears. "You were caught in the crossfire. Nothing personal, Mia."

Rage hits me. "Nothing personal? You couldn't have made this any more personal if you had tried. You see, Martin, there is something you don't understand. You just see that your family left you, abandoned you. You don't see the fact that you were brought into Hudson's family, he had no idea who you truly were and yet he brought you into the fold. He trusted you, and you betrayed him. Who is the bad guy now?"

He takes another step toward me and pushes me into the wall, I wince in pain.

He begins to pace, I'm relieved that he's walked away from me. "I should have been the boss!" It's the same thing with him over and over again he doesn't quite grasp the fact that while Hudson's father is part of the reason he became the boss. It's not the entire reason, he became the boss due to the depth of him. His character is what makes him the boss.

"You're mad at Harrison and you have taken it out on everyone else. You have lost every friend you have ever made.

He shrugs he doesn't give a fuck. He's so lost in revenge, he doesn't care.

I sigh and move on. "Did you shoot Marline?"

He smirks. "She was getting too close. I couldn't let her find out what I was doing."

"You didn't mean to kill her though, you only shot her in her arm. Unlike my mom where you shot her multiple times you only fired the gun once at Marline. You really love her." It's a statement, I don't need him to answer because I already know the truth. "You would have killed her if you didn't."

"Shut up!" He screams at me, I'm getting too close to the truth.

"She's been the one to tell you everything about us and our lives. How did you manage to get her to do that?" The way Hudson talks about her and from the little that I know about her, she's extremely loyal to Hudson.

He looks pleased with himself. "It was easy, she had no idea I was playing her. Tell me something Mia, when you and Hudson are lying in bed together do you tell him everything he wants to know?"

Pillow talk. I knew Marline didn't mean it. Where the hell is Hudson? I haven't heard Harrison make a sound since Martin broke the office door down, is he okay?

"She'd hate you knowing that you twisted everything she told you and used it against those she cares about." I tell him and I instantly know it's the wrong thing to say.

His eyes darken and he lifts his gun, pointing it at me. "You have no idea. You're naive, haven't you learned yet,

Mia? Everyone has an agenda and Marline is no different." My eyes close, and time seems to slow down as I wait for him to shoot me.

Bang

The sound reverberates around the room.

SIXTEEN

Hudson

I COULDN'T LET anyone else drive, I needed to get to Mia. My foot was pedal to the metal for the entire drive. My rage is taking over me and I'm ready to kill. This bloodthirstiness is something I haven't felt in a long ass time. It's back in full force and I'm going to let it consume me, just as soon as I have Martin in my grasp.

David had my phone on while I was driving, we were watching everything unfold in the house. We watched as he shot my dad, heard him baiting Mia to come out of the office or my dad would die. I've never been so proud of my girl. She kept her cool and stayed hidden. She did exactly as I had asked. When that fucker splintered my office door I knew that there wasn't much time left. I was three minutes out and I needed to get there sooner rather than later.

I listened to every word he said to her. God my fucking woman is amazing, she kept him talking, I watched as she backed herself into the wall but she still kept talking to him as though she wasn't afraid. She found out everything I wanted to know from my mom. Mia was right, mom had no idea that he was using her. I get that she's pissed that we are going after the man she has feelings for, but she has to realize that he has killed people close to us. There's no way he's ever getting away with his life.

David, Aaron, and I are quiet walking into the house, not wanting to alert him that we are here. Rory is outside checking on Coby, Dylan, Ronald, and Cormac. Thankfully as I passed them I did a glancing sweep of them all, each one of them have shots to their arms, none are life threatening.

As we enter the house, I see Jagger on the floor, a gunshot to his arm, he's losing blood but he's going to be okay. He's sitting up and alert. As soon as he spots us, he gets to his feet. As we sweep through the house he follows us. Aaron stops and checks on dad, he's got a gunshot wound to his right thigh and one in his gut. He's pale and sweaty, it's not a good sign.

Mia tells Martin that mom's going to hate him when she finds out that he used her. I watch in slow motion as he lifts his gun and points it at her, telling her that she's wrong, that my mom knows a lot more than Mia thinks. I don't even hesitate, I lift my gun and raise it at the back of his head.

Bang

I fire a shot, watch as Martin goes down, crashing to the floor with a loud thud. My eyes are on Mia, her face etched in pain. I'm moving toward her as she slides down the wall.

"Mia talk to me!" I demand, I can't get to her quick enough.

"Hudson something is wrong," she cries, her hands rubbing her bump. "Pain in my stomach." She's finding it hard to talk, like the breath has been taken from her.

"Is it the baby?" I question as I reach her.

She nods. "He's not moving, and I'm in so much pain," she whimpers.

I clench my jaw as I see the blood on her pants. "Where have you been shot?" I ask her just seeing the blood is making make me lose my mind.

She frowns, deep lines form in his forehead. "I haven't been shot."

What the hell? "Mia, you're bleeding. Where are you bleeding?" I search over her body, trying to find where the hell the blood is coming from.

She glances down between her legs, a blood curdling scream erupts from her lips. "Hudson, our baby!"

"Get a fucking ambulance!" I yell, I thought I knew what fear was when Mia was taken, but nothing compares to this right now, knowing that our baby is in trouble is unlike anything I've ever felt before.

"Hudson!" Mia cries, tears rolling down her face. "Is the baby okay?"

I need to tamp down my fear, it's not helping anyone. I swallow it back and wipe away Mia's tears with my thumb. "Hey, Princess everything is going to be okay. We're going to get you to the hospital. Don't worry." Even though I say the words to calm her down, I don't believe them. She's almost seven months pregnant, it's not good, it's too early.

"We never said what you wanted to call him." She's talking in the past tense, that sounds like he's gone.

I shake my head, never wanting to hear her say that ever again. "Mia, he's going to be okay. You are going to be okay. We are going to get you to the hospital, and get you checked out. This is probably stress don't worry, just take deep breaths." Fucking hell, everything is not okay but there's nothing else that I can say right now.

She gives me a tired smile. "I love you so much." She's panting, sweat coating her brows.

I pull her into my arms. "Princess, I love you too."

"Boss, ambulances are on their way. They're two minutes out. Coby called them when we arrived," Aaron says, I have no idea where the hell he is, nor do I give a fuck. My focus is right where it should be, on Mia.

"Is your dad okay?" She pants, her gaze going to the door.

"Look at me, Princess," I tell her, not wanting her to see my dad right now, he's not in good shape and seeing him could make her worse. She looks at me, worry clouding those gorgeous eyes of hers. "He's doing okay, you two will probably be next to each other in the hospital."

"They'll need to make a wing for everyone here," David laughs at his own joke.

Mia's eyes widen. "Did he just make a joke?"

I shake my head. "Yeah, it's very rare but he does make them. Although they're not that great." I'm glad that she's focused on something else than her pain right now.

"Is he dead?" she questions, her face is no longer etched in pain as it was when she was going down the wall. Her breathing is no longer labored, I want to see if she's bleeding but I don't want to move her. Waiting for EMT's is like waiting for an eternity.

"I don't know, and honestly I don't care. After everything that asshole has done he deserves to die." I tell her, glancing back and seeing that fucker lying flat on the floor. He hasn't moved since I shot him, then again, I'm not surprised. My aim is fucking true, I never miss my target.

She hums. "Is your mom doing okay?"

There is something about this woman, she always manages to catch me off guard, she always says something I wouldn't expect her to in a time where most would panic.

"She's angry," I bite out. She shouldn't be fucking angry with me.

She grins. "Let me guess, you're pissed that she's angry at you and you think she should be angry that she was played."

I ignore her smug smile. "Right now I'm focusing on you. The quicker the EMT's get here the better."

She narrows her eyes at me, her lips pursing into a thin line. "Hudson, you better not be rude to the EMT's. They're going to try and help us, they don't need you making the job harder.

"As if I would." They just need to hurry up.

"They're here, as are the cops," Aaron shouts and relief washes through me, and of course the fucking cops are here.

"Deal with the cops, if they want to talk to me, they can follow us to the hospital," I say loud enough for everyone to hear.

"Hudson." Mia glares at me. "Please be nice," she asks and I nod just as the EMT's rush into the bedroom.

"She's bleeding and she's twenty three weeks pregnant," I tell them, and watch helplessly as they assess her and load her onto a gurney. Blood rushes to my head as I watch them wheel her past me.

"Hudson?" Mia calls out in a panic, her hand in the air as she tries to find me.

"I'm here," I tell her, my hand gripping hers.

"Don't let go," she pleads with me, "Please."

"I'm not going anywhere, Princess," I promise her, I turn to look at David and Aaron. "Sort this shit out, then meet me at the hospital." They nod in unison as I leave the office still clasping onto Mia's hand.

"Boss?" The deep voice pulls me from my thoughts. I turn to find David standing in the doorway. "The cops want to talk to you."

I nod, I knew it would be only a matter of time. I'm surprised they waited this long. Thankfully Mia's sleeping and the doctor has been by to check on her. They're monitoring her tonight and tomorrow and see if the bleeding has stopped. If it has, we should be okay, but if it continues, then there's a high probability that Mia will go into labor.

I place a kiss against Mia's head and walk out of her room. "Who is it?" I ask as David walks beside me.

"Spinelli."

Good, it's someone on my payroll. Not that there's much they can do. Yes, I shot someone, but that person had shot five people beforehand and had a gun pointed at my wife.

"How is everyone?" This is the first time that I've left Mia's side since we arrived in the hospital.

"None were hit anywhere fatal. Your dad's probably going to have to stay in a couple of days, maybe longer. He lost a lot of blood, but he'll be fine. How's Mia?"

"She's okay, she's not getting pains anymore nor is she bleeding. The doctor says she had a placental abruption. We're going to have to see how tonight and tomorrow goes before we can say for definite, but at the moment things look okay." She needs no stress and bed rest. That's exactly what she's going to get.

Spinelli and his partner Tanor are waiting for me outside the hospital entrance. "Sorry for pulling you away from your wife, but we really need to get a statement from you." Spinelli says. "How is your wife?"

"She's doing okay. Can we get this over with?" I want to get back to her before she wakes up.

He nods. "Of course. Can you please explain what happened today?"

I grit my teeth. "This bullshit, I'm sure you've already had everyone and their mother tell you what went down today. Why do you need me to reiterate everything you already know?"

Tanor sighs, "Mr Brady…"

"I understand you have a job to do, but this is just overkill. You have everyone's statements. I got home to find my men shot and that fucker with a gun pointed at my pregnant wife. I shot him before he got the chance to shoot her. He is dead isn't he?" I have to double check, that fucker's like Houdini.

"Yes, Mr Brady, he's dead," Tanor says, the corner of his lips turning up as he tries not to smile.

"Are we done?"

Spinelli nods. "Yeah Hudson, we're done. I wish your wife a speedy recovery."

"Thanks." I nod as I turn on my heel and walk back into the hospital.

"Boss, is there anything you need from me?" David asks, his voice tight.

I stop walking and look at him. His eyes are dark, the way they go when he thinks of his wife. "No, you've done more than enough for me, David. Take some time, however much you need."

He nods. "In your debt," he grunts.

"No, you're not."

He glares at me. "I'm in your debt."

I shake my head, he's not going to listen to me no matter what I say to him. "Go, and David, I meant what I said. Take as long as you want." He pats my shoulder as he walks past me. I walk toward Mia's room, relieved that this shit is all over. There's only one thing left for me to do and that's talk to mom.

Mia's eyes are on me as I enter her room, she's wide awake and I'm wondering when she woke up. "Where did you go?" Her voice thick with sleep.

"I had to talk to the cops, it's done now. How long have you been awake?"

She smiles. "It's over?"

Sitting down on the bed beside her I take her hand. "Yeah, Princess, it's over. That fucker isn't going to hurt anyone ever again."

Tears form in her eyes. "Thank God." She leans forward and presses a kiss against my lips. "How is everyone?"

"They're good, no one is going to die. Dad's got the longest recovery. He lost a lot of blood. He'll be fine though."

"Are they all still here?"

I frown. "I think so, why?"

"I want to say thank you. They risked their lives for us, Hudson."

"I'll check and see if I can get them here." I get to my feet and place a kiss to her cheek. "Do you want anything?"

She shakes her head and winces a little. "No, I'm okay, thank you."

"Are you in pain?"

"No," she replies and I narrow my eyes. She sighs. "Not like you think, I've got a headache and when I shook my head it hurt. I'll be fine."

I glare at her. "If it doesn't ease, I'm calling the doctor."

"Hudson, I'm fine."

"Mia, I'm not taking any chances. If it doesn't ease in

the next twenty minutes I'm calling for the doctor." She nods at my words.

Walking out of her room, I'm surprised to see the men standing outside. "You okay?" I ask them in general.

"Yep, fucker couldn't shoot straight," Coby says with a smile.

"I'm good boss," Cormac says as Dylan and Roland nod their agreement.

"It'll take a lot more than a bullet to stop us. Your dad's fine, he's annoying the hell out of the nursing staff. He wants to go home," Jagger informs me.

"Mia wants to see you all." Aaron and Rory take a step backward. "Oh no, she wants to see you two as well." I smirk at their shocked faces.

"How is she doing?" Jagger asks as the men walk in ahead of us.

"She seems to be okay, the next twenty four hours are crucial. She had a placental abruption. The doctor said it isn't severe, it's less than two centimeters. The pain is gone, so we're hoping that she'll be able to carry the baby to term."

"Fuck," he whispers. "Thank fuck that asshole is dead."

"A-fucking-men," I mutter as Jagger and I enter the hospital room. The men are standing around waiting for Mia to say something, she's staring at them with tears in her eyes. "Princess?"

She shakes her head. "Sorry," she whispers, "Jagger," She says with a fond smile, "Aaron." She looks at him, she loves him just as she does Jagger and David. He cares for her just as much. "Rory, Cormac, Ronald, Dylan, and Coby." Her smile grows with each and every name. "Thank you. From the bottom of my heart, thank you."

"We're just doing our job ma'am." Dylan says shrugging, his cheeks heating.

Mia shakes her head. "No, your job is for Hudson. You went above and beyond for me. Each one of you got injured." She glances at Aaron. "Thank you."

Aaron shakes his head. "You're family, Mia, so we'll protect you just as we'd protect anyone else in this family. Besides, you're carrying our nephew."

"Mia, this is what we do. Not only was that asshole after you, he killed a lot of people. We weren't going to let that happen to anyone else," Jagger tells her and her tears begin to fall. She'd managed to hold them off for a while.

"I'd do it again in a heartbeat," Rory says.

"Yep, you're the sweetest chick ever," Cormac tells her and I smirk. "Do you think anyone else would bring us here and thank us?"

"This is a lame thank you," Mia tells them, "I wish there was a way I could repay you all."

"I heard you make a good meal," Cormac says and dodges his brother's slap to his head. "What? It's true. I heard she's a great cook."

"Bro, now isn't the time." Rory murmurs.

Mia laughs, I love that fucking sound. "I'll cook dinner for you all," she promises them.

"After the baby's born," I tell her, and she glares at me. "Mia, you're on bedrest until he's born."

"That's our cue," Rory says and the men start leaving, all except Cormac. "Cor?"

"What, the good stuff is happening." God, this fucker is pushing it.

"Bro, you don't get involved in a domestic. Especially one that's with the boss. So move it." Rory pushes him through the door.

Mia smiles, but as soon as the door closes behind the men her smile fades. "Where's David?"

"Mia, the man is hurting, has been ever since his wife

died. He pushed everything aside until we finally got this fucker. Which we did today. Now that Martin is dead, David's taking some time."

"Oh, do you think he'll be okay?" She's worried about him, I am too. "How long is he going to be gone?"

"I don't know, we just have to let him heal, Princess."

"Yeah, we all need time to heal," she tells me softly and lays down in the bed. "Hopefully, he'll be okay," she murmurs, her eyes slowly closing.

"Sleep baby. I'll be here."

SEVENTEEN

Hudson

"BUT..."

"No buts Mia, you need to rest. It's too early for you to go into labor. So it's bedrest until the doctor says otherwise." I lay her down on the bed and pull the covers over her.

She huffs in annoyance. "Fine, but I'm not happy about it."

I smirk. "Yeah, you've made it clear."

"Are you going to talk to your mom today?"

"Yes," I say through clenched teeth, she's been asking me that same damn question for the past four days. "She's been calling me nonstop. Dad's pissed, he wants to be here when she is as he has more questions than I do."

Her eyes widen. "Oh. Is that wise having him here when she is?"

I shrug, it's funny, before all this shit happened, I'd have been on Mom's side always but right now, I'm on Dad's. "Yes, he deserves to know."

She nods. "Yes he does, but Hudson, your mom's hurting."

I grit my teeth, I'm sick of fucking hearing that shit. "I know she is, but Mia she's fucked up and she needs to own up to that shit."

"Can I be present?"

"Hell no," I reply instantly, "Mia, you're meant to be resting, not being around stressful situations."

"Please?" She begs. "It's not going to be hard on your mom and your dad. I know that if I'm around they won't be too hard on one another."

She's right, both of them aren't as angry when Mia's around. She's a soothing balm on everyone around her. "Fine, but your ass sits on the sofa and it doesn't move. I don't give a fuck if you need to use the bathroom. You ask and I'll carry you."

She bites her lip, I know she's dying to argue with me.

"Either that, or you stay right where you are."

She sighs, "Fine, you win. I'll be good and stay on the sofa."

Good. "Do you need anything?"

She glances at the stack of magazines that Sarah bought over for her. Along with six books, Mia's eyes lit up when she saw them, she told me she hadn't read in a while. "No I'm good thank you."

"I need to make a phone call, I'll be in the sitting room so if you need me all you have to do is yell okay?"

She nods. "I'll be fine, I'm not an invalid, Hudson. Besides I've got a lot of reading to do."

"Okay, I won't be long." I need to call Aaron and see if he's heard from David, he was going to check in on him. He's also sorting out the new shipment that's due in this evening.

Walking into the sitting room, I hit dial and listen to the ringing.

"Boss." Aaron greets me.

"Have you spoken to David?"

"Yes boss, he's currently in Texas, he's flying back tomorrow."

"Good, is everything set for this evening?" I've never let Aaron handle one before. It used to be Martin and then David, Aaron was the only other person that I'd trust to do the job, besides Jagger but he's pulling back a bit. Sarah went a little crazy when she heard he was shot. Thankfully she's calmed down a lot and he's easing his way back into things.

"Yes, I have the men ready and a diversion or two in place should we need them. I'm not going into this blind. I have everything planned out. Don't worry boss, I won't let you down."

I have no fucking doubt that he'll do the job, I wouldn't have asked him if I hadn't. "Call me if you need me."

"Sure Boss, but I won't. Mia needs you."

I laugh. "I'm already driving her crazy."

He chuckles, "Boss, you were doing that before she was released from the hospital. Back then she had the nursing staff as a buffer. Now she has to deal with your crazy ass twenty-four-seven."

I shake my head, he's right. I'm a tad overprotective but for good reason. "Right now, I don't give a shit. Mia's and the baby's health are the most important things and if I have to tie her to the bed then so be it."

His laughter increases. "Oh God help her."

"So expect phone calls or text messages asking for help."

That stops him in his tracks. "What am I meant to do if I get one of these SOS's?"

"As long as she's resting, I don't give a fuck."

"Okay boss." He sounds a little terrified, and I'm pretty

sure it's not down to me but of what Mia's going to ask him, if she contacts him.

"Call me if you need me."

"Will do boss. I'll call you once it's done."

I end the call just as the doorbell rings. As I put my cell back into my pocket, the front door opens and in walks Dad. He's walking with a limp, he's still sore from the gunshot wounds he's got. The one to his gut giving him the most pain, he's threatened to kill Jagger numerous times. Jagger has made it his mission to tell as many lame ass jokes as he can, trying to make my dad laugh, knowing damn well that it hurts like a bitch when he does.

"Is Mia settled in?" he asks, no hey son, how are you? Not anymore.

"Yes, she's in bed. She's asked to be present when mom gets here and I agreed. She's to sit on the sofa and not move." I'm telling him because he'll make sure she stays put.

He nods. "I'll sit beside her."

"No you won't, you'll take one of the armchairs, I will sit on the sofa. I want you far away from mom as possible."

His eyes narrow into slits. "Fine. The sooner she gets here the quicker we can get this shit done."

He's not the only one. I want answers and then I want to forget that Martin ever existed, that fucker has caused enough pain and suffering to last a lifetime. "Mom should be here any minute. Let me get Mia."

"I'm getting a beer."

I shake my head. "Make yourself at home why don't you. Get me one while you're at it."

"Boy, when did I become your slave?"

"Since you're in my house helping yourself to my beer."

Walking into the bedroom, I see Mia sitting there, her

entire face lit up with the smile she has, she has a book in her hand and opened. She's been reading, why on earth do I find that sexy?

"Dad's here."

She nods. "I heard. Is he okay?"

"Yep, he's helping himself to some beer. We're waiting on mom to arrive." I take the book from her hands and place it down on the nightstand. "He's still sore." I tell her before she can even ask.

"Is he taking his pills?"

I give her a 'what do you think' look as I pull the comforter off of her. "He's never taken drugs, it's just not something he'll ever do." I lift her into my arms. "There's no point in saying anything."

"Your mother's here," Dad calls out and Mia's eyes widen at the anger in his tone.

"Hey Harrison, hey Marline," Mia says as I place her down on the sofa. Dad grabs the blanket off the chair and passes it to me.

"How are you feeling?" Mom asks her, sitting down on one of the armchairs, Dad takes a seat on the opposite one.

"I'm better, glad to be home."

"That's good. How bad is Hudson annoying you?" Mom laughs at her own words, pissing me off in the process.

I reach for the beer that dad left on the table for me as Mia pulls the blanket over her and gets comfortable beside me.

"She wouldn't be in this situation had it not been for you and that fucking boyfriend of yours," Dad bites out.

Fucking A, we're starting early.

"How is it my fault?" she asks naively.

"Dad," I warn, I know him too well, he's about to go in on her.

"No Son, I've waited long enough for this shit."

Mom waves me off. "Let him say whatever it is he's dying to say."

I sit back against the sofa and let them at it.

"Since when did you become so stupid? Not your fault. Marline, it is your fault. You were sleeping with the fucker. Especially after everything he'd done. You told him everything about those closest to you." Dad's utterly disgusted. As much as he and Mom's marriage never worked, he actually respected her a hell of a lot, well until now that is.

"I never knew that he had hurt Mia."

"Bullshit," I say through clenched teeth, pissed that she's even saying that shit. "You fucking knew."

Mom's face hardens, she knows that she's fucked up.

"You damn well knew what that fucking asshole did to Mia, you heard everything Marline so don't bullshit us with that shit that you had no idea. You just didn't want to believe that he could do that. At least be fucking honest." Dad's tone is one of barely contained rage.

"Yes, I believed him when he said that Mia was mistaken."

Mia's hand rests on my leg, my mom's basically called her a liar to her face and she's comforting me?

"When did you become so gullible?" Dad's face is scrunched up in disgust. "You went against your own son, and you have the nerve to call me a bastard."

"Mom, you've fucked up. You helped that murderer kill even more people, and you can't see what you've done." It's as though I'm talking to a wall.

She crosses her arms over her chest and sits back in her seat. She's not saying anything.

"This is getting us nowhere," Mia says. "Marline, I

know you never intended telling him things, but you trusted him. You placed your trust in the wrong person. We're all guilty of doing that."

Mom's face falls and I see the guilt written all over it. "I should have known."

"Maybe, I think Hudson believes that you chose Martin over him."

Her eyes widen. "I never."

"You chose to believe Martin over Hudson," Mia explains softly. "Your judgment was off and that's what you need to apologize for. You need to make us understand why you chose to believe him."

Fuck, how can Mia put it so eloquently?

"I was stupid," Mom replies. I've never heard her be so vulnerable before.

"You were in love," Mia responds. "I understand that, hell we all do. You were blinded by love and by doing so you hurt your son. You have to make amends for that."

She instantly nods. "I will, I've messed up and I'm going to spend the rest of my life making up for it."

"You hurt Harrison..." Mia begins.

Mom cuts her off. "He hurt me."

Mia shakes her head. "I understand that you were hurt but Marline, he told you from the very beginning how your marriage would be. Did he lie to you?"

Mom thinks about it for a while, her jaw tensing as she shakes her head.

"He cheated on you multiple times, I can't imagine how that made you feel but Marline, he fell in love with my mom after you fell in love with Martin. Don't you think that's got to hurt? Hmm? That was his son you were sleeping with."

"I didn't set out to be with him. In fact, I pushed him

away for a very long time. I knew who he was from the very beginning."

Mia shifts in her seat and I glance down at her, she looks worried. "Mia?" I question, wondering what's going on.

"Marline, did you tell Martin where my mom was?"

I close my eyes as I hear dad's sharp intake of breath. Fuck.

"I'm so sorry, Mia."

I open my eyes and stare at my mom in horror. Why the fuck would she do that?

"Marline, I have no words." I can hear the tears in dad's voice. "You went too far. What did Tina ever do to you?"

Mom's eyes flash with anger. "She took you from me."

I've had enough of this shit. "Mom." My voice is hard. "She didn't take Dad from you. You were fucking Martin long before she came along. Why did you tell him where she was?"

She shrugs. "I never intended for him to kill her. We were talking about your father and her, how they were separated, I told him that Tina was living in the motel."

"How did you know where she was staying?" Dad demands and it's a good question, not many knew where she was living as her and dad were in the midst of getting back together.

"I met Martin across the street from the motel, I watched her go into her room."

"So you fucking told him?" Dad growls. "What the fuck is wrong with you?"

Mom's eyes widen. "I'm sorry, okay? I never meant for this to happen."

"What did you think would happen when you told that fucking psychopath where she lived? That he'd bring her fucking biscuits?" Dad's angrier than I have ever heard him before.

Mom shakes her head, as she wipes away her tears. "I don't know, it was in passing."

"What else did you tell him? Hmm? We obviously know you told him that Mia was pregnant."

"No, I never told him that."

I sigh. "Enough with the lies mom, there's no other way he could have known."

"Hudson, I'm not lying. He knew before I did." As crazy as it sounds, I actually believe her.

"So how?" Dad asks. "There's no way he could have known unless he was dumpster diving or got access to her medical records."

"I don't know Harrison, but it wasn't me," she cries. "I know that you may never believe me but I'm telling the truth. I'm sorry for my stupidity, for the hurt that my actions have caused. It was never my intention for this to happen."

"What good is that now? He killed her, he killed my wife because you were fucking jealous." Dad gets to his feet.

"Jealous?" Mom questions, a deep furrow between her brows.

"Yes Marline, jealous. You hated Tina because I left you for her. You were jealous because I loved her when I never loved you."

Mom scoffs. "You are a pig Harrison." She doesn't deny that she was jealous of him and Tina.

"Stop," Mia cries, her tone strained. It must be hard to hear this shit, her mom died and dad and my mom are arguing like Mia's not in the room.

"Mia..." Dad says, his eyes soften when they look at her.

"It's over Harrison. Mom's gone and as much as you'd love to hate Marline, she didn't do anything wrong. She had no idea that Martin would kill mom."

"Exactly, Tina is gone."

Mia shakes her head, "She is and she's not coming back. My baby is never going to see her. So I need you to put your differences aside and get along. You have a child together and we're going to have your grandchild, you're going to have to get along."

Dad sits down again, he looks winded. "Mia..."

Tears form in Mia's eyes. "I know, it's going to be hard but I'm going to need you, both of you, in our lives. I would really appreciate it if you both could be civil. I know Hudson would too."

Mom nods, "You're right, we need to sit down and talk, clear the air properly and then hopefully we can be civil."

Dad releases a heavy sigh. "Fine, name a time and a place and I'll be there."

"Tomorrow, stop by my house around four. I'll cook dinner and we'll talk," Mom says as she gets to her feet. "I'm going to go now, Hudson, thank you for allowing me to talk and explain my side of things. Mia," Mom's voice cracks at her name. "You are truly an extraordinary young lady. Your parents would be so proud of you. Thank you for your support." She bends down and places a kiss against Mia's cheek. "I'll see you soon. Take care and rest."

Mia smiles, "I will do. Hope everything goes okay tomorrow for you both."

"Harrison, I'll see you tomorrow." Dad nods at her words, he's still not in the mood for forgiving her and I can't blame him. I'd probably be the same if the tables were turned, she made him out to be the bad guy all along when she was just as bad as he was.

"I'll call you tomorrow Hudson," she tells me and I nod. "I'll see myself out."

I take a sip of beer, it's getting warm. The front door closes and dad instantly relaxes.

"I can't believe you Hudson," Mia says with a growl.

"What?" I ask in disbelief, what the hell have I done now?

"Your mom poured her heart out and you didn't even get up and say goodbye properly. You were extremely chilly with her."

"Mia, you can't expect things to be as they were," Dad tells her. "She's lied. You have to realize that Marline is a manipulator, she's finally shown her true colors. She's got a long way to make amends, and one conversation isn't going to help."

I pull her body into mine. "He's right, Princess, but don't worry, mom and I are going to be fine." They're not going to be the way they were before but I'll be civil to her just as I used to be to dad. "Do you want to stay here for a bit longer or do you want to go to bed?"

She smiles. "Stay here. Also, I'm hungry."

Dad chuckles. "As am I. Boy, what are you making us?"

I shake my head, damn these two are as thick as thieves. "I'm ordering take-out." I leave them to talk, knowing that they're both hurting right now. There's only one person that can put a smile on my dad's face and that's Tina, or talking about her. My cell rings and I see it's Colby.

"Hey man, what's up?"

"How's Mia?" He asks, and I bite back my smile. She's wormed her way into everyone's hearts.

"She's okay." I don't think she'll be out of my sight ever again.

"That's good. I found Martin's laptop, the fucker

hacked Mia's medical records, it's how he found out she was pregnant."

Mom was telling the truth, fuck. "Did you find anything else?"

"So much fucking shit on your dad and Tina, but nothing on you. Thank fuck he's dead."

"A-fucking-men to that."

"I'm still combing through his shit, if I find anything else, I'll let you know." He tells me and I don't envy his job at all. Martin was a sick fuck and I can just imagine all the shit he's going to have to look through.

"Thanks." I say and end the call.

I hear laughter from the sitting room and the pain in my chest eases. They're safe, that's the most important thing, that fucker can't hurt her anymore.

EIGHTEEN

Mia

T̲w̲e̲l̲v̲e̲ ̲w̲e̲e̲k̲s̲ ̲l̲a̲t̲e̲r̲

"MIA," he murmurs, as his hand rests on my bump. He's waiting for the baby to move. Our little boy is like clockwork, nine am and he'll start dancing. "I know that you have a name in mind. Every time I suggest one you act disinterested."

"I'm not disinterested, I just want to meet him first." I do have a name in mind but I'm not sure what Hudson will think of it. So until our son is born, I'm not saying a word.

"Okay, he's having a lazy morning," he comments when the baby doesn't move. "Want some breakfast?"

I nod. "I can make it," I tell him sitting up.

"No, I'll make it, go have a shower and it'll be ready when you're ready." He gets off the bed and reaches for the sweatpants that are lying on the floor.

I smile at him. "That sounds heavenly, thank you."

He winks at me. "Don't thank me Mia, you're my wife, I look after you."

Since I've been home from the hospital, he's been so

attentive. He's delegated a lot more of his work so that he's home most of the time. I know that's because he's worried about the both of us, but also because he's able to breathe now that Martin's gone.

We've been lucky, the tear wasn't as bad as I had thought and I've had bed rest since I've been home. It's boring and I've gone stir crazy but I've done it because it gave my baby the best chance of coming to full term which is three weeks away although the doctor said if he was born soon, he'd be okay, as I'm thirty-seven weeks. We're almost there and I'm grateful that we've got this far, each day that passes gives him more chance of survival. My nerves are kicking in now, I'm scared for the labor. It's the fear of the pain that's going to come.

I slowly get out of bed, Hudson's cell is ringing in the background somewhere. It's weird, now when his cell rings I'm not fearful for what's about to come. Walking to the bathroom, my hand reaches out and I hold onto the wall as a twinge of pain hits my stomach. It hits me hard and takes my breath away. Just as quick as it comes, it passes again.

Gingerly getting into the shower, I can hear Hudson on the phone, it's probably his mom. She calls him every day, it took a while for him to forgive her, and even longer for Harrison but they've done so and their relationships are stronger than ever before. Marline and Harrison have been getting along and I'm curious if something has happened between them. The loving glances that she gives him are a far cry from how she would have looked at him only a few months ago.

I cry out as pain hits me once again. Shit, the baby hasn't moved and I'm getting pains. Does that mean I'm in labor? It's too early, I shouldn't be. I should call Sarah, she'd know what this feels like. I wait until the pain passes before climbing out of the shower. I've never had a pain take my breath away so quickly, the fear I had about the labor has intensified. Wrapping a towel around me, I go into my bedroom and sit down on the bed. Reaching for my phone, I dial Sarah's number.

"Hey Mia," she says chirpily

Sarah and I are able to spend more time together now that there's no longer a threat to my life. It's been good to spend time with her again, and also be around Allie, that girl has grown so much and I love her more and more each day.

"Sarah." I gasp as another pain hits me and I feel a popping sensation, glancing down at my legs, I see water running down it.

"Mia?" she calls, "Mia are you okay?"

"I'm not sure," I breathe, "I keep getting pains in my stomach."

"Mia are you in labor?"

"No, I don't think so, it's too early. Sarah, the baby hasn't moved this morning." I tell her as tears slowly fall.

"Oh Mia, you need to go to the hospital. Now," she demands, I can hear the worry in her voice.

"Okay, I'm going to get dressed and I'll have Hudson drive me." Water is still trickling down my legs, it seems to be getting heavier.

"No," she shouts. "I'm going to get Jagger's mom to watch Allie and then Jagger and I are coming to you and bringing you to the hospital. Hudson's going to be a mess when he finds out you're in labor, you don't want him driving."

Jagger chuckles in the background. "He's going to lose his damn mind."

"Mia, deep breaths okay," Sarah instructs me. "I'll be there soon. Get dressed and wait for us."

I get to my feet. "I will, thank you." I take a deep breath as pain hits me again. "Oh," I whisper as the water gushes down my leg now. "Sarah, I think my water has broken."

"Don't worry Mia, Jagger's mom is on her way now. We'll be there soon."

"Okay." Tears fall faster as my stomach tightens once again and pain hits me.

"Breathe Mia, breathe," she tells me.

I cry out as the pain intensifies. "Sarah, it hurts." Tears are streaming down my face. Where the hell is Hudson?

"I know Mia, I know. It'll be over soon, I promise." She sounds as though she's crying too. "Oh, Jag's mom's here. We're leaving now. I'll stay on the phone and talk to you."

I shake my head, even though she can't see me. My feet are soaked, as is the floor. I need to clean up. "No, go, I'll see you soon."

She sighs. "Okay Mia, I love you. I'll be there soon."

"Love you too." I hang up and throw my cell onto the bed. "Hudson." I yell, hoping he's in the kitchen and not his office otherwise he's not going to hear me.

I get no reply. Thankfully my water seems to have stopped. I quickly waddle over to the wardrobe and take one of my maternity dresses off the hanger. I throw it on, not bothering with a bra. Once I'm dressed, I waddle over to the cupboard and take out a couple of towels. "Hudson?" I call out once again but still no reply.

Kneeling down, I start cleaning the mess I made. Pain hits me again, once again taking all the oxygen from me. I try and remember the breathing techniques I learned while doing Lamaze classes but for the life of me I can't seem to remember them. It takes me a while to clean up, I throw the towels into the laundry basket and walk into the hall. The kitchen and sitting room are quiet, making my way toward the office, I have to stop as once again pain hits me. Once the pain passes, I stand for a couple of minutes to catch my breath.

I open the office door, Hudson's sitting behind the desk, the phone tucked between his shoulder and his ear as he types on his computer. He glances at me, a deep frown on his face. "Aaron, hold on a second will you?" There's an edge to his tone. "Mia, what's wrong?"

I walk toward him. He's focused on me, his eyes never leaving me. "Hudson, Sarah and Jagger are on their way."

His frown deepens. "Okay, is everything okay?"

My hands reach for the chair as pain hits me once again. "Ahhhhhhh." This one is worse than any of the one's before. I close my eyes as I wait for the pain to pass. They're coming almost every ten minutes. I need to get to the hospital.

"Mia!" Hudson calls out, I can hear his feet moving but I don't dare look at him. "Princess, talk to me," he whispers, his hands on my face.

Opening my eyes, he's staring at me, searching to see what's wrong. "Hudson, he's coming," I breathe once the pain has gone.

The color drains from his face, he shakes his head. "Mia, it's too soon. Are you sure?"

My eyes widen. "Hudson, my water broke and I'm having contractions. Of course I'm sure."

His thumbs caress my cheeks. "Mia, I don't mean to be an ass. It's too soon."

"I know, Jagger and Sarah are on their way. They're driving us to the hospital."

He kisses my forehead. "Okay princess." His arms tighten around me, I rest my head against his shoulder, loving his protectiveness.

"We haven't got the crib for our room ready yet," I whisper against him.

"Don't worry, it'll be done. David and Aaron will do it."

I raise my head. "David's back?" I smile, I've missed him. Even though he's usually silent, he's one of Hudson's men I really like.

"Yeah, baby he's back. He's with Aaron right now."

David was due back a couple of months ago but he found out something's about his wife that devastated him. It was then that I was worried about him the most, he stopped checking in with everyone and had gone radio silent. I honestly believed he'd never return.

"Is he okay?"

Hudson smiles. "Yeah baby he's okay. He's better than he's been in a while. He's come to terms with everything that's happened and what he learned about his wife." The way he says his wife isn't great, he knows what happened or what was unveiled and he won't tell me. It's not his place to say.

"Hello?" I hear yelled and relief washes through me. Sarah and Jagger are here.

"Come on princess, let's get you to the hospital." He holds onto me as we walk out of the office.

"Don't forget to get the bag." I've had it packed for the past six weeks. It's by the door so we'd know where it is for when we needed it.

"I've got it Mia, Jagger's already putting it into the trunk," Sarah says as we walk towards her.

"Thanks." I smile but that smile soon vanishes as pain hits me once again. "Ahhhhhhhhhh." I scream as the pain intensifies.

"Breathe Mia," Sarah instructs me and I do as she says. "That's it, in and out," I copy her and I'm able to not panic.

"Thank you." I say to them both as they help me out of the house and toward the car.

"Don't thank me Mia, you did the same for me."

I smile. "You never got me into this situation." I raise my eyebrows at Hudson who grimaces.

"Shit, I'm glad I wasn't there for Allie's birth." Jagger laughs but I know that he's joking, he'd loved to have been there.

"Try not to break Hudson's finger," Sarah jokes and I watch as Hudson visibly blanches.

"Jeez, you doing okay Mia?" Jagger asks, a horrified look on his face.

I nod as Hudson helps me to get into the car. "Yeah, I can't wait to meet him," I reply to Jagger.

Hudson climbs in beside me and holds my hand. "It's going to be okay."

My hand rests on my bump. "Hudson he's not moved." I gently rub in hopes that it'll get him to move.

"He's okay, he's just waiting to finally come out. We'll be at the hospital soon. Please try and relax," he tells me but I can hear the worry in his voice.

"Relax?" I question, "I'm about to have at least a six pound baby come out of my vagina. Don't tell me to relax," I say through clenched teeth.

Jagger laughs. "Dude, if you value your life, keep your mouth shut. Mia once you've had the baby, the pain will be forgotten."

"You weren't even present at your child's birth, how the hell do you know that?" Hudson asks in disgust.

It's Sarah's turn to laugh, "I'm obsessed with One Born Every Minute. I've made Jagger watch them with me. He seems to think that just because he's watched them it's made him some sort of expert. Ignore him."

"So it's not true? You don't forget about the pain?" I ask, everything I've read or heard says that you do forget.

She turns to face me, glaring at Jagger as she does. "Oh that's true, you do. Within seconds of Allie being born I couldn't remember how bad the pain was. Watching you have your contraction brought it all back. I don't envy you right now." She's got a big smirk on her face.

"You're not helping," I say through clenched teeth as once again I'm hit with a contraction.

"Mia, we're almost here. Keep breathing." Hudson whispers as he rubs my back trying to sooth me. "Less than five minutes. You're doing amazing."

I lean my head against him once the pain goes. "God, why do women do this to themselves more than once?" I've not even had the worst part yet and I'm already swearing off having anymore.

"Fuck if I know," Hudson mutters.

"Sex," Sarah says simply, "If the sex is out of this world, you're bound to get pregnant. It's like laws of physics or something."

Hudson laughs, "No it isn't."

She shrugs, "Well it should be. You get a world shattering orgasm, then boom you're knocked up."

"World shattering?" Jagger smirks.

"Oh I never said I had one. I just said if you had one then you should be. There's a difference."

I bite my lip so that the laughter doesn't bubble up. Hudson however doesn't hide it. He chuckles making Sarah smile wider.

"Did you get a world shattering orgasm?" Hudson whispers to me as Jagger pulls into the Hospital grounds.

"Each and every time we have sex." I tell him honestly.

"Oh jeez, why did you tell him that? It's going to go to his head. That's something we don't need." Jagger quips.

"Jealous because I know how to please my woman?" Hudson fires back.

"Okay enough, we're here." Sarah says as Jagger pulls up outside the hospital entrance.

"You can't park there," someone shouts.

Hudson's head spins to glare at whoever said it. "My wife's in labor, where the hell would you like me to go?" His voice hard.

"Oh, um, I'm sorry Mr Brady." The man stutters.

Hudson ignores him. "Jagger, I'm taking the girls with me, you park the car and come back and find us after."

Sarah looks relieved. "Thank you," she says to Hudson.

"She wants you here, I need you here. You keep her calm, I on the other hand will lose my damn mind if she's in pain and can't push through it," Hudson replies and I smile, it's true, he'll probably threaten to kill someone if they don't help me.

They help me into the hospital and up to the maternity ward. Just as we reach the midwife my contraction hits.

"Breathe, Mia." Sarah instructs. "She's having contractions every six minutes now, her water has broken, and she's only thirty seven weeks. The baby hasn't moved this morning," Sarah informs the midwife. "In and out Mia." She tells me and once again, I'm able to push through it.

"Okay Mia, we're going to bring you into the room and see how much you've advanced." I nod, my hand gripping Hudson's tightly, it's all so real now.

Once I'm into the labor suite I'm dressed in a hospital gown and the midwife is checking to see how far I'm dilated. She makes a humming noise in the back of her throat and instantly I'm on edge, that's not a good sound to make. "Mrs Brady, you're only two centimeters dilated. I'm going to call the doctor to have a look at you." She reassures me but there's something about the way she's unable to meet my eyes that makes me scared.

"What does that mean?" Hudson asks once the midwife is gone.

"She needs to be ten centimeters for the baby to come." Sarah tells him and Hudson pales. "Don't panic, she'll be ten centimetres before you even know it."

That doesn't placate him, he begins to pace the room.

The doctor comes in and immediately walks over to me. "Hello Mrs Brady, I'm Doctor Nola, I'm the OBGYN here. How are you feeling?"

"Like I've got a baby ready to explode out of me," I quip.

Doctor Nola laughs, "It'll be over soon. I just need to do a quick check and see where we go from there, okay?"

I nod, that uneasy feeling returning in full force. Something is wrong, but they're not saying what.

"Okay Mrs Brady, your son's heart rate is quite low and as you're only two centimeters dilated, we're going to have do an emergency caesarean."

My mouth instantly dries. "Is he going to be okay?"

The doctor immediately nods, "The quicker we can get him out, the better."

"Okay, can my husband come with us?" The nurse begins putting a cannula into my arm and someone else enters the room.

"Mrs Brady, your husband is encouraged to come along with you. To be present when your son is being born. We're going to give you an epidural and get the OR prepped."

I'm listening to what he's explaining to me, everything that's going to happen but I can't focus. My mind is in overdrive as I watch what's happening around me.

Within ten minutes I'm lying on an operating table, my

lower body numb from the epidural and Hudson standing beside me.

"Mr and Mrs Brady, are you ready to meet your son?" Doctor Nola asks and we both nod.

I glance at Hudson, trying to think of anything but what's happening down below. Hudson's eyes are the most expressive I've ever seen. But when they widen and shine brightly I know that he's seen our son.

A cry rings through the room and my breath catches, God, he's okay. If they cry that is a good thing. Isn't it?

"Congratulations, Mrs and Mr Brady, your son is doing well," Doctor Nola says as the nurse places our baby onto my chest. "He's going to need some oxygen, but he's otherwise fine."

Tears pool in my eyes as I stare at my boy. "Thank you." I whisper to Hudson, so grateful to have him in my life, for giving me this miracle.

"Thank you Princess, you have given me the greatest gifts in life. You and our son." A tear falls down his face and he doesn't even wipe it away as he stares at our boy. "Okay Princess, what's his name?"

I smile, "David Aaron Barney Brady." Jagger's going to be his Godfather so I know that he won't be upset that he's not named after him.

Hudson nods immediately. "It's perfect," he comments before placing a kiss on my head.

I feel so content holding David in my arms as Hudson places a kiss on our son's cheek. I can't wait to show him off to the world.

"How is she?" The question rouses me from my sleep.

"She's a fucking trouper," Hudson replies.

Opening my eyes I see that I'm surrounded by our nearest and dearest. Sarah, Jagger, Harrison, Marline, David, Aaron, Rory, Cormac, Coby, Ronald, and Dylan. "Hey," I croak.

Hudson turns to me. "You should be asleep."

I shake my head. "I'm fine. Is he still asleep?"

"Yeah, he's been stirring for the past ten minutes so he'll probably wake soon." And as if on cue the baby starts crying.

"Here Mia, I have the bottle ready," Sarah says, passing me the bottle and a burp cloth as Hudson gingerly reaches for baby David and passes him to me.

The feel of this beautiful miracle in my arms is the best thing in the world, I never thought I could be this happy.

"Congratulations, Mia," Jagger says with a smile.

"Thank you," I whisper as I hold David against me, giving him his bottle.

"What's his name?" Harrison asks and I look to Hudson.

"We have something to ask first," He says, he's worried that Jagger may be pissed about us not naming David after him so he wants to ask him and Sarah to be David's godparents first. "Sarah and Jagger, will you be his Godparents?"

They both nod immediately, Sarah has tears falling down her face. "I'd be honored." Jagger says gruffly.

Back slaps and handshakes go around the room congratulating them on being David's godparents.

"We've chosen his name. I think it suits him perfectly." I tell them and a hush goes over the room. "Meet David Aaron Barney Brady." I say with pride.

Harrison hoots, "I love it. It's perfect."

"It really is." Marline says with a fond smile as she looks at her grandson.

I turn to look at both David and Aaron, they both look dumbstruck.

"I love it Mia," Sarah says, "Jagger and I are going to go. We'll be back tomorrow." She places a kiss on my cheek, followed by one on baby David's head before hugging Hudson.

"We're going to go too," Harrison says and my eyes widen. "Now before you get upset. Today is for you and Hudson, I'll be back bright and early in the morning."

"He's right, congratulations both of you, thank you for giving us a grandchild."

"My pleasure." And it is, I'm so in love with him.

"See you tomorrow," Harrison says and leaves Marline, Roland, Dylan, Rory, and Cormac following behind. Leaving David and Aaron behind.

"I don't know what to say," Aaron says, he's still in shock.

"There's nothing to say. I will never be able to repay you for what you have done for me. The way you both risked your lives for me, for us," I tell him holding David a little closer to me.

"I never wanted repayment. I'd have protected you anyway." I stare at him and he shakes his head. "Fine, debt repaid." He shakes Hudson's hand before giving me a kiss on his cheek. "You're one in a million Mia, Hudson got lucky finding you. I'll see you both tomorrow."

"David?" I ask once Aaron leaves, he's standing there with a shocked look on his face.

"Fucking hell." He breathes. "I've been dealt shit for the past four months and the only bright spot was you and now you do this."

I glance at Hudson who's got a smile on his face. I have no idea what to say. "Hudson agreed to it."

"Of course he did, but it was your idea. If Hudson was

given the choice he'd have named him something beginning with H, like Harleson."

"Watch it," Hudson warns him.

"Are you okay? I missed you." Hudson rolls his eyes at my words.

"Better now, thank you. Keep going Mia, you'll give Hudson something to think about." He winks at me and I laugh, there's no way Hudson would ever think that. "Honestly, I'm good. I really appreciate what you both have done for me. I'm forever in your debt." He smiles at us both, turns on his heel and walks out of the room.

Hudson sits on the bed beside me, while I burp David. "Love you, Mia."

I rest my head against his chest. "I love you so much." I have my entire world on this bed and it feels amazing.

Epilogue

Hudson
Eighteen Years Later

"HALEY BRADY, get your ass back here right now," I yell.

Lorna and Maya giggle on the sofa.

David, Dennon, and Finley walk into the sitting room, all of them not happy.

"Mom!" Haley yells, she sounds as though she's going to cry.

The sound of feet pounding on the stairs tells me that Haley has gotten her way and Mia's on the way down.

"Sitting room now!" Mia's voice is just loud enough for us all to hear. Lorna and Maya's giggling has stopped and my boys sit their asses down on the sofa beside their twin sisters and wait for their mom and sister to come into the room.

"Mom's pissed," Dennon comments and I glare at him. He shrugs, "What? She is."

"Yeah and so would you be if you had to deal with all of you and your stupidity," I fire back.

"I'm not stupid," Finley says and David chuckles.

"Of course you're not sweetie." Mia says softly and I smirk.

"See at least someone agrees with me."

Mia smiles. "Yeah, stupid isn't someone who gets their head stuck down the toilet," her tone filled with sarcasm.

Something that's lost on my son. "Thank you," he says with a smile.

"Mom, are you okay?" Dennon asks, he's a mommy's boy. He'll do anything and everything for her, just like his dad will.

"No, I'm not." She takes a seat beside me and huffs, she looks tired. "I'm trying to put your brother to sleep and all we can hear is your sister and father screaming." She turns to glare at me. "He cries, you're going to settle him." My eyes widen before I slowly smirk. "Hudson, this isn't funny."

"No baby, I never said it was."

Her eyes narrowed into slits. "So why the hell are you smirking?"

"What's going on?" Finley asks.

"Mom's pregnant again," David responds, shaking his head.

"Eww." Haley says and I sit back in my seat and smirk when Mia spins her head to glare at our oldest daughter. Thank fuck I'm out of the hot seat.

"Eww? I'm not even forty yet Haley," Mia says affronted.

Haley takes a step back knowing that she's skating on thin ice. "Mom, I didn't mean it that way, just eww that you and daddy are still doing it."

"Doing what?" Lorna asks curiously.

I turn to my eight year old and her twin sister. "Nothing that concerns you."

Maya scrunches her nose up, "I bet it's kissing. They're always doing that."

"Anyway," Mia says changing the subject. "Want to tell me where you're going?" She asks Haley.

"I told you mom, I'm going to the mall."

Mia's eyebrows practically hit her hairline. "Dressed like that?" She points at the tiny belt that Haley calls a skirt and a tank top that doesn't even cover her stomach.

She puts her hands on her hips, she's so much like her mom. "Everyone wears these."

"Only the slutty ones," Dennon murmurs but we all hear him.

"Dennon!" I yell.

Mia shakes her head. "Apologize to your sister now."

"I never called her one."

"Dennon," Mia's tone is full of anger. "You're grounded for two weeks."

"What? That's unreasonable," he says outraged.

"Three weeks," Mia returns.

"Mom!" He doesn't learn, never argue with Mia, you won't win.

"A month." She's daring him to continue.

"Bu..."

"Dude, shut up." David elbows him in the gut.

"Finished?" Mia asks and Dennon nods. "Good, now Haley, do you think I was born yesterday?"

Haley thinks about her answer, smart girl. "No mom, I know you weren't but I'm really going to the mall."

"With who?" I ask, she's not fooling anyone with her innocent act.

She crosses her arms over her chest, "Cassie, Maria, Taylor, and Allie."

"Oh shit," Dennon mutters. "You're throwing Allie under the bus."

David's eyes flash with anger but he doesn't say anything. There's something going on between those two but neither of them are saying anything.

"You want to go to the mall?" Mia asks and Haley nods. "Then go upstairs and change."

"Ugh!" she cries, "Fine, I'll go and change."

"Good, then your father can take you and your sisters to the mall." Mia smiles sweetly at her.

"Oh daddy, we're going to the mall?" Maya asks excitedly whereas Lorna looks annoyed, she's her father's daughter. Hates the mall just as much as I do.

"No, we're not," Haley says. "I hate you." She narrows her eyes at me and I shrug, I've heard it a hundred times before. The first time stung like crazy but now I'm used to it and she only says it when she doesn't get her way.

"You want to spend time with Taylor?" Mia asks and I glare at her wondering where the hell she's going with this.

"Yes," Haley says solemnly.

"Then invite him here and you can watch a movie."

Haley's eyes light up, "Really?"

Mia nods. "Yes but in here with the door opened."

Haley jumps up and down on the spot and rushes over to hug Mia, "Love you mom." Before rushing out of the room to no doubt call that asshole Taylor.

"Why did you invite that moron here?" I ask and the boys laugh.

"Because I'd rather have them here under our supervision than for her to sneak out and meet him, or her lie to us about where she's going."

"Mia, that's not going to happen."

She smirks at me, "And how was it that we met again?"

"Fair point. You are to stay with her," I tell my boys. "He doesn't get to touch her."

Mia stands up and shakes her head. "I'm not part of

this, I'm going to make dinner. Lorna, do you want to help?"

"Yes mommy." She wiggles off the sofa and rushes out of the room behind Mia.

"Maya baby, go help your mom."

She glares at me as she gets off the sofa. "You're so sexist dad. You never ask any of the boys to help."

"Why are all these females full of attitude?" I ask wondering when my baby girl started back chatting me.

"I can hear you!" Mia says, "And your daughter is right. You've never once asked the boys to help me do dinner, you always make the girls." She doesn't have any heat in her voice.

"They are to be separated at all times," I instruct my boys.

Dennon and Finley smirk, enjoying the task that I've set them. "On it dad." Dennon replies, he's fourteen and thinks he's God's gift to women. Mia tells me that he takes after me but I don't see it. Finley is the calmer of my boys, he's so laid back. But he'll knock you out with one punch if you piss him off enough. He's thirteen and takes after his mom looks wise.

"Dad, can I have a word?" David asks and I nod for him to follow me.

Sitting down in my office I wait for him to spill whatever is on his mind. "I know that you and mom spoke about me finishing school and college first before joining the family."

"Yeah," I say carefully wondering where he's going with this and why he's not having this conversation with his mom as well.

"I don't want to go to college, in fact, once I graduate I want to join the family." He graduates in less than two months.

"What's brought this on?"

He shrugs. "I've been thinking about it a lot. All of us want to join the family."

"All of you?"

He nods. "Yeah, Haley, Dennon, and Finley."

"Have you spoken to your mom about this?"

"Yeah dad, I told her earlier today and she told me that it was my choice as I'm eighteen now. She'd prefer it if I went to college but she can't stop me from doing what I want. As long as I'm happy then she is."

"That sounds like your mom alright. So what do you want?"

He sits up straighter. "One day I want to be the boss, just as you are, just as gramps was before you and your gramps was before him."

"Your name doesn't mean you're the boss."

He nods. "I know, mom's told me about it. She's told us all about it. Gramps told me how you worked your way up and that's what I want to do too. The respect your men have for you was earned and if I'm going to be boss one day then I want to earn it too."

I nod in approval, that right there shows me that my son has what it takes to be boss. "Okay then, this weekend you're with me."

His eyes light up like I've just told him all his Christmas' have come at once. "Thanks dad."

"We done?" He nods. "Good, we're going to help your mom and sister's out with making dinner."

"Okay, thanks dad for listening and for the opportunity."

I get to my feet. "It's going to be hard work, a lot of grunt work."

He smiles. "It'll be worth it."

I pat his back. "You'll be fine, Son."

When we walk into the kitchen Mia's gaze comes directly to me. "He's going to make a great boss, Princess."

"Yeah, I know, I've known for a long time. He's the younger version of you, Hudson."

"I'm fucking proud of my kids," I tell her pulling her into my chest.

"I am too," she whispers.

My hand rests on her stomach. "Just as we will be proud of this one too."

"This is the last one Hudson."

I smile, she said that the last time.

Seven months later, Morgan Brady was born, she was followed ten months later by her brother Lewis.

The End

All the ways you can follow Brooke

Website:
https://brookesummersautho.wixsite.com/website

Newsletter:
http://eepurl.com/gC1j8P

Join Brooke's Babes:
https://www.facebook.com/groups/BrookesBabes/

Books By Brooke
―――――――――――――

The Kingpin Series:

Dangerous Secrets

Forbidden Lust

Forever Love

Printed in Great Britain
by Amazon